AF076556

DEAR SATAN...

NEW YORK TIMES BESTSELLING AUTHOR
EVE LANGLAIS

Copyright © 2021, Eve Langlais

Cover Art © Dreams2Media 2021

Produced in Canada

www.EveLanglais.com

E- ISBN: 978 177 384 2523

Print ISBN : 978 177 384 2530

ALL RIGHTS RESERVED

This book is a work of fiction and the characters, events and dialogue found within the story are of the author's imagination and are not to be construed as real. Any resemblance to actual events or persons, either living or deceased, is completely coincidental.

No part of this book may be reproduced or shared in any form or by any means, electronic or mechanical, including but not limited to digital copying, file sharing, audio recording, email and printing without permission in writing from the author.

FOREWORD

'Twas the days before Christmas
    And all throughout Hell,
    Perversion was happening,
    Crime was up as well.

The babies were alive,
    And not killed in their crib,
    His wife was acting normal,
    Which meant good sex for him.

Satan wore his red latex,
    And Gaia her skimpiest thong,
    When Polkie arrived
    With a letter sent wrong.

1

"The mail, Your Eminence." Polkie—short for Philokrates, a strange looking mix between a gremlin and Atlantean, wearing a proper all black suit to match his expression—placed a tarnished tray stacked with letters upon the Devil's desk. Red, pink, some covered in drawings and stickers of line art holiday trees or fat snowmen and fatter Santas. Some had that damned glitter that got into everything.

Evil shit. It's why the creator of it currently suffered. The devil should never sparkle. That was for vampires.

"Christmas letters. My favorite." He rubbed his hands. While he publicly complained about

Christmas—all that kindness and family time and goodwill blah blah puke—secretly he loved it.

The month of December, leading up to his nephew's birthday, was a busy time, what with all the increased crime and the drama amongst adults. Divorces skyrocketed. Violence, too. So much sin it was hard to keep track at times.

Christmas also meant thousands upon thousands of letters being mailed by children to the North Pole and that fat bastard who didn't even live there. So many letters and some addressed to Lucifer himself.

Dear Satan.

He read each and every one. He could predict the future for a few with their greedy demands. Some didn't ask for toys but acts that guaranteed he'd see them eventually. Pretty much everyone past the baby stage ended up crossing the Styx.

Polkie set the tray down, the stack of mail so high that when it toppled, it covered Satan's massive desk. So many letters. He wiggled his fingers over the pile, trying to choose the first one.

"You look like a hungry pervert," remarked his wife.

Gaia sat knitting spider webs, fresh from the spinneret glands, while their two youngest played in the corner. Junior fired live rats at Lucifer's giant, meat-eating Venus meat trap while Jujube giggled and clapped. Daddy's little hellions. Wait until they saw what he'd got them for the most horribly amazing holiday of the year.

Hating Christmas led to him taking steps to ensure it got ruined. However, his efforts were nothing compared to what one Nikolas Claus accomplished. Turning it from Charlie's—formerly known as Jesus—birthday into a thing with its own set of decorations, happiness, joy.

Gross.

Lucifer fought back, introducing the greed aspect as people asked for more and more, turning it into a commercial event. A parody of what it used to be and a moneymaker that sent sin spinning off the charts. Christmas brought out the greedy bastards in his life.

"I am hungry to bask in the love of my fans." He stroked the pile of letters.

"They're not your fans. You stole Santa's letters. Again," Gaia stated without stopping her stitching. Her fingers flew, the needles clacking away, making who knew what. Didn't matter. He'd tell her it was wonderful because not even the devil was dumb enough to piss off his wife. Why just last week he'd been reminded of this lesson when she asked him if she'd gotten fatter and he said he liked the new curves.

Wrong answer.

The Bahamas got their first deep freeze, which everyone blamed on climate change. Idiots. As if she cared about pollution. Gaia had a way of cleaning up her planet. But when it came to her temper, Lucifer was the one causing havoc with storms and temperature increases. He knew how to get her hot.

"It's not stealing if they're addressed to me," he declared. He even had the fine print to prove his point.

"Fine, I'll give you they say Satan, but it's the wrong address. We don't live in the North Pole."

"Not true. I have a mailbox there."

She stopped knitting. "You're doing it on purpose to justify stealing those children's wishes from Santa."

"Don't be blaming me for the fact they can't spell." He blamed the public education system. Today's youth were woefully incapable of matching his wits. It wasn't even any fun anymore making truly lopsided deals for human souls.

"You should do the right thing," his wife declared. "Give them to Santa."

The very idea. Lucifer choked and grabbed his chest. "You trying to kill me, wench?"

"Just saying it doesn't have to always be about you."

Was she new? "But it *is* all about me."

Her gaze narrowed, and she injected a warning tone. "Luc."

"What is it, my wench?"

"Those letters belong to children."

"I am aware of that fact, and as you well know, I would never hurt a child." He did have standards after all. That said, once they became adults, all bets were off.

"There are different kinds of hurt. Like destroying their belief in the real Santa."

"Bah, hellbug," he exclaimed, huffing smoke. "You're nitpicking!"

"I better not find nits," she said with a glare at her spinning spiders. who quivered and shot out a useless gob that made her sigh as she snapped the thread and tied it off. "Aren't you busy enough without stealing Nick's mail?"

Nick now, was it? As if he needed another reason to be stubborn. "Never too busy for my fans." Lucifer didn't get as many letters what with the postal service and their difficulties delivering to the first ring of Hell. Apparently, neither rain or snow didn't extend to brimstone and hellfire. Pussies. The rare few that made it to his mailbox didn't make it past his hellhounds.

"Fans?" She snorted.

"You're just jealous."

"Not really. I prefer actions to words. My fans show their love with tree plantings and luscious gardens. By protecting wetlands. And the carbon tax."

Lucifer snorted. "The carbon tax is a scam created for yours truly." He was quite proud of the way he'd managed to make the rich even richer.

"You are reprehensible."

"I know." He winked. "And yours are dicks."

"They are not!" she huffed.

"I've seen how they show their appreciation. Ever increasing plastics in your ocean. The mowing down of rainforests. The smog." Oops. Too late he shut his mouth, closed his eyes, and waited for her to smite him.

When the expected smiting didn't occur, he opened one eye and saw her calmly knitting. "Um, not gonna argue?"

"As if I'd argue with you over something so silly." She tittered.

Uh. Oh.

She was pissed.

An itch began in his manly parts. A really bad itch that turned to burning.

"Ouch!" Lucifer hopped out of his seat, dug around inside his trousers, and ripped free the silken boxers she'd knitted for him. They smoked into ash as they dropped to the floor. He proffered the mightiest of glowers.

As usual, his wife didn't appear impressed.

"You were saying?" was her smug reply.

"I'm saying it's time I started going commando again. Let the boys roam free. Be the sexy demon you first met." He swung his hips.

She rolled her eyes. "That move has never been, and never will be, sexy."

"Worked on you."

"Actually, your saving grace is that tongue. Who knew forked could make such a difference?" She winked.

Lucifer would have dropped to his knees to worship her if not for a knock at his door—and the damned children. Forget the olden days where he fucked her anywhere he could, even if there was an audience. Now he had to wait until they could be private. It did make the fast romps in closets and hidden spots more exciting.

"Are you going to answer that?" she asked as someone rapped again.

"Me?" he exclaimed. "The devil is not a servant. Opening doors is Polkie's job."

"Actually, no it's not. We have a new butler."

"No, we don't."

"Given Polkie is getting up there in millennia, I've hired him some help," Gaia stated as if this was okay.

"An apprentice! I didn't approve this." He glowered.

"You told me to run the household as I see fit and to not bother you with annoying questions."

"I meant those fucking paint chips. and you know it. One hundred shades of cream you made me look at." And look as he might, he couldn't see the differences as she went on and on and on about the varying hues.

"Forgive me for thinking you'd want a say in the décor for our bedroom."

"I don't give a flying fuck about the colors of the walls or the thread count in the sheets so long as you're naked in bed with those delicious toes up around my ears." His leer had dropped countless panties in his lifetime.

Gaia was the one woman who didn't succumb. She came to him on her terms.

It was so damned sexy. And annoying.

"Your intent doesn't count, only your words." She snapped her fingers and suddenly wore reading glasses on the tip of her nose. She held up a sheet of paper. "Here's the conversation in question. Would you like me to read it to you?"

"It's as if you are trying to goad me into a fight." Meaning she wanted sex. Makeup sex. The best kind after sweet, and then there was impromptu and languorous…

"According to the transcript—"

He interrupted. "Yada. Yada. Fine. I said it. You want to hire people. Go ahead. But don't come crying to me when you hurt Polkie's feelings and shit starts going wrong." There were few people he dared piss off. Polkie being one of the. That guy knew how to make his life miserable without getting caught doing it.

"I think the person gave up on knocking," she stated, putting away her glasses. For now. He'd be asking her to wear those later, maybe with some heels and nothing else.

"Mustn't have been important." He waved a hand. "Tell me more about this new butler."

"Well, he's handsome for one."

Before Lucifer could change that by adding a few barnacles and maybe another eye, a sudden whoosh of soot puffed from the hearth, causing a cloud in the room that had him closing his eyes for a second while he waved his hands to get rid of it. When Lucifer opened them, he discovered a visitor standing in his office.

An unwelcome one at that. His cousin.

The one and only Santa Claus.

2

"You know, most people use the door to visit me. Those people live," Satan muttered with a scowl as the big man brushed off his red suit.

A suit Lucifer envied. He could have had his own made and worn it with panache. However, people would think he'd copied the do-gooder Santa Nikolas Claus.

Unacceptable. People copied *him*.

His cousin's apparel was modeled after that of the Santa from the Netflix special, *The Christmas Chronicles*: red duster—using pleather because killing animals was cruel, blah blah blah—lined in fake fur. His boots shone so well they acted as a mirror. Lucifer truly envied Santa's beard. He could do scruffy, but full-on bush from his chin? Patchy at best.

Cousin Nick had brought his famous bag with him. It acted as an inter-portal conduit to his workshop, which wasn't actually in the North Pole as people thought but on another planet. Pluto to be exact. Cousin Nick was banished there a few decades ago because of his Krampus phase. He'd apparently earned back his visiting privileges.

"Hand them over," his not-so-jolly cousin demanded.

Lucifer was never clear on which side of the family Nick fell. It had been a long time since their birth. They'd both changed a lot since then. Some of them for the better. Others—ahem, his cousin—got more annoying each year.

A good thing Lucifer was king when it came to being a dick. "A fine hello to you, too, my dear cousin. Judging by your increased girth, your flushed complexion, and that irregularity I detect in your heartbeat, your wife is still trying to kill you."

Everyone joked about how Mrs. Claus kept feeding her husband sugar and fat in an attempt to get rid of him. Not a joke. She really did want him gone. Why she didn't just use a sword and sever his head to save herself the trouble was something Lucifer had discussed at length with her over spiked eggnog. She grumbled about the promise she'd made during their wedding vows about not harming her husband. She also wouldn't cheat.

People with morals were just distasteful to Lucifer. It was why he didn't visit often.

Nick cupped his belly, full of beers and nachos. not jelly. "You're just jealous of my Becky because your wife can't cook."

Gaia laughed.

Laughed at the insult, because she and Nick went way back.

She wagged a finger. "Naughty Nick. You know what happens when I cook. A little bit of this, a little bit of that, and we end up with the blobfish."

Nick snickered. "Those were ugly but not all your cooking went bad. My elves are still one of your greatest accomplishments."

Gaia had performed some tricky splicing to create a species that thrived in the cold and were possessed not only of long lives but an extremely good work ethic. Elves truly were happiest when busy. Nick and his crew got things done and delivered without fail every Christmas. Brought joy and happiness all around the world.

And the family called Lucifer the disgrace.

"I remember us making the elves." She sighed dreamily. "Good times."

Wait a second, did she ever get that look when she thought of him? Did she like Nick more?

Ridiculous. Still, his wife's past with his cousin and continued friendship annoyed. "Why are you here?" he barked.

"You know why. My mail." Nick headed for the desk. "I'll be taking those."

Lucifer leaned back in his seat, laced his hands over his flat belly, and smiled. "Touch them and lose that hand. Permanently."

"They're not for you."

"Not true. They're addressed to me."

"Satan Claus?" Nick cajoled. "We both know that's not your last name."

"Actually, it is."

"Since when?" Nick blustered.

"Since I applied for a name change. It is a little bit lengthier now. Satan Lucifer Morningstar Yahweh Kardashian Skywalker Manson Easter Bunny Claus Baphomet and a few more." Nine hundred pages worth.

"And what of the address?" Nick argued.

"That's what I said." His wife took the cad's side.

"You're not the only one with a mailbox in the North Pole." Turned out a few people had some redirects. Santa Claws, a grumpy cat living in San Francisco who inherited a billionaire's fortune. Then there was Satan Claws, Lucifer's massive and demonic cat who used the shreds of his letters to line his kitty litter box.

"Those letters are for me," Nick insisted.

"I disagree. Let's read one, shall we?" Lucifer grabbed the most promising one from the pile. Black envelope, the red marker almost impossible to read. Addressed to Satan. Inside, a scribbled note. "Dear Satan. I've been doing my best to be bad all year, but I'm worried that's not enough to earn me a spot in Hell. How can I sin more this stupid, commercialistic holiday season? Signed Adam." Lucifer tossed it aside. "For starters, he shouldn't have to ask. How hard is it to break laws and do no good?"

"You planted that!" Nick accused.

As if he'd admit to cheating. "Don't be a sore loser."

"I'm not the one who set the board game on fire when I was winning."

"You intentionally snuck that serpent in there to sabotage me." Snakes and Ladders. The most evil game in creation.

"Still such a baby. Can't admit I beat you," Nick taunted.

For a moment, Lucifer saw red and his nostrils smoked. Just what Nick intended, judging by his smirk.

Lucifer composed himself and then retaliated. "Sounds to me like you're jealous that my wife still likes to suck my dick every night."

He ducked the needle Gaia threw at his head. Totally worth it to see his cousin red cheeked.

"You're a pig."

"Demon, actually. And you're not."

Cousin Nick might be old, but he was a youngster compared to the devil.

"You want the letters. Keep them. I can always find more children to replace them." A statement that had Nick turning and holding out his arms to Lucifer's kids.

"Who wants to sit on Santa's lap?"

As if—

What the ever-loving fuck! Lucifer almost exploded as Jujube crawled over and bounced on her bum, exclaiming, "Santa!" She clapped and held out her arms.

Traitor.

"Naptime!" Lucifer snapped his fingers and sent both children off to the nursery.

The lie fooled no one. Nick got a smug expression, and Lucifer's ire grew. He began entertaining thoughts of revenge, which interfered with his previous plans that involved getting into his wife's panties. The distraction couldn't be allowed to happen.

His wife needed him to defile her. He couldn't let anything get in the way of that.

Time to get rid of this pompous fool. Jolly his ass. "Don't you have some elves to crack a whip on? Some reindeer to fellate into flying? A wife to disappoint?"

"I'll leave once you hand over *my* mail." Nick imperiously held out a hand.

"Still no, and before you argue, you don't have a case. Ask my lawyer."

A woman in a blue dress suit appeared at the snap of his fingers. Kourtney—who usually worked earth-side for his match making service, Grim Dating—scowled as she crossed her arms. "What now?" Such a lovely attitude and to think he could enjoy it anytime he wanted since he'd arranged to have her fall for one of his Grim Reapers.

"I have need of your legal expertise."

Kourtney arched a brow. "And what did we say about proper notice?"

"You spoke. I never agreed. And even if I had, I would have been lying." Lucifer could never understand how people didn't grasp this simple concept.

"It's a good thing you pay me ridiculously well," she grumbled. "What is it this time?"

"Letters addressed to Satan Claus. Does my cousin have a legal right to them?"

Kourtney sighed. "No. But morally—"

Lucifer cut her off. "That's enough. Dismissed." He waved his hand and made her go away then turned to his cousin. "You heard the lawyer."

"We both know you don't really want them, so what will it take for you to give me that pile?" Nick pointed to the tray.

"I'm so glad you asked." Lucifer offered his terms, to which Nick laughed so hard his cheeks turned rosy.

They negotiated, and even before Nick left with the mail, Lucifer was pondering who to evict that he might demolish their home to enlarge his garage for his upcoming new sports car. Elven made, which meant more surprises than a 007 vehicle.

There was a knock. Knowing it was Polkie, Lucifer flicked his fingers and opened the door.

"Your Highness, it would seem we misplaced one of your letters." Polkie waved a red envelope.

"Misplaced?"

"The new butler dropped it."

"This kind of ineptitude is unacceptable." Lucifer shook his head.

"I agree, sire. I shall have my understudy punished at once."

"Borrow my kitsune of nine tails if you require," he offered. The electricity in it shredded flesh like a knife through soft butter.

"Too generous, sire."

"Don't worry, I'll add years to your sentence to pay for it."

"Hmph." Polkie handed over the letter before departing.

Being a woman, which meant observant and nosy, his wife said, "Looks like another one for Nick."

"No, it's not." It was addressed to Satan.

"You just made a deal—"

"For the pile on my desk. Nothing more." He was very specific in with his terms.

"You are so crooked," she muttered.

"I am." He prided himself on it. "Would you like me to read it to you?"

"Listen as you shatter some poor child's dream?" She shrugged. "Okay."

"That's my wench. Ahem." He tore open the envelope and began to read. "Dear Satan…"

3

Dear Santa.

Merry pursed her lips and stared at the word. Nope. That wasn't right. Rather than waste paper and hasten the demise of their beautiful planet, she crossed it out and started over.

Dear Satan.

Much better.

Her tongue poked from between her lips as she wrote.

I don't want anything for Xmas.

A lazy way of spelling but her dyslexia had a problem with the longer version. She reread and then crossed it out because the phrase wasn't quite true. She did want something. Something huge.

For Xmas, I'd like to see my boy smile.

It had been almost a year since she'd last glimpsed one. A year since she'd heard Miguel speak. He'd retreated into a tiny shell of himself since the incident that saw his dad dead. Poor traumatized baby. It broke her heart.

Which was why she had to do something about it. If only she weren't running out of ideas.

Buying the biggest teddy bear ended up in her almost suffocating under its weight, as Miguel insisted on dragging it to her bed every night for a snuggle. He might not be able to express it aloud, but he showed his love in his own way.

But that was all Miguel gave her. Nothing brought a smile. Not the old Looney Tunes characters falling off cliffs or whacking each other with giant hammers. Not that cat who liked to sit in their apartment window licking its butt.

Since his dad died, not even a hint of a smile graced his lips.

When motherly methods failed, she'd attempted more extreme measures.

For Valentine's Day, she tried offering flowers and chocolates to Cupid. Left a note promising anything in return. Cupid swiped left.

Easter? She'd left some of her famous Buffalo chicken casserole for the bunny, only to find out he was vegan in a scathing note left behind.

Mustering up her courage, she'd stripped and danced around the May pole. All that happened was a mosquito bite on her ass.

A naked jig at Halloween around a bonfire, while fun, hadn't brought the devil. She found out later it was because his wife insisted on monogamy.

During it all, she'd prayed to God but understood he might be angry at her. She'd not been able to attend a service since getting pregnant with Miguel. She projectile vomited the moment she stepped foot on church property.

Once Miguel was born, Merry was fine, but her son went into violent spasms whenever she got near holy ground. Must be some kind of weird magnetic effect. She stopped going and prayed at home. It didn't appear to have any effect. Miguel was a shadow of his happy boy self.

I need a Christmas miracle. And she knew of only one person who could help. She kept writing her note, tip of her tongue between her lips, as she concentrated on the letters she had to write.

He's a good boy.

Miguel was the best of sons, but his mother? Much as she tried, she sometimes couldn't seem to help being bad. Why, just the other day, rather than wait in the rain with Miguel for the next bus, she ignored the man in the lovely, probably expensive suit behind her who would probably need to have it dry cleaned because of the weather. She could have offered he get on the bus first, but she knew this bus would have little room at this hour. And it was raining.

She felt horrible about her selfishness. Would it be held against her? It was said Santa knew when you were sleeping, awake, bad, or good. Her request would probably go into the trash bin. But still, she had to try.

Please help me.

She frowned. It didn't look quite right.

Merry wrote beside it. *Help Miguel.*

She bit the end of her pen. Should she cross the previous part out?

And make the letter an even bigger mess?

Nope. She'd leave it as is and mail it before she changed her mind.

Asking Santa for help. The nerve. Especially since last Christmas she'd forgotten to put out cookies what with being in the emergency room all night.

No excuse. She was probably on the naughty list forever now.

She sealed her note in an envelope and then carefully labelled it Satan. She skipped his last name since she couldn't remember if it was spelled with a K or a C. But she knew the rest. 666 Igloo Street, North Pole. OHOHOH.

Funny the things a person remembered. Especially since she had no idea why she knew Santa's address.

"It must be fate." She hummed happily aloud before she popped it into her purse to mail. Then she turned a bright smile on Miguel. "Let's make some cookies."

Her son didn't say a word. His face remained solemn, and yet he rose from the floor where he'd been paging through a picture book on trucks. They entered the tiny kitchen, and he opened the cupboard and pulled out a shaker of candy sprinkles.

"You want to make sugar cookies so we can decorate them?" she asked.

His reply was to head for his chair at the kitchen table. Her heart melted.

"We are going to make the bestest cookies ever! With icing, too!"

She didn't get a smile but did enjoy watching him lick the mixing bowl. It was a good day.

They didn't run into trouble until she pulled out the box of Christmas stuff later that night.

4

Satan, the red-dicked devil,
  Had a very shiny trick,
  And when he used it on Gaia,
  Flooding hit the town of Wrick.

"I swear I won't be responsible for the maiming if you continue that bawdy poem in front of our children." Gaia glared.

"Only you can hear it, wench." And later Lucifer would remind her of its truth.

After they ditched the kids.

Currently, Junior rode on Lucifer's shoulders while Jujube travelled on her mother's hip. Family stroll to see the dogs.

"Perhaps instead of indulging in tavern songs, you could explain why you're not passing on that woman's letter. I thought you learned your lesson the last time you stole Nick's mail and decided to actually answer it," Gaia harangued.

"It wasn't that bad." Getting imps to make gifts for children had its advantage. Free labor being the main one. The problem being the toys tended to be cursed or possessed or both. Lucifer might be many things, but he didn't torture children. The innocent shall not suffer.

But the wicked…the wicked were his to play with forever.

"You made three of those kids you answered that Christmas into orphans."

True, but on the flip side, those who died? Shit parents. What Gaia didn't know was he ensured the orphans were adopted by well-off families with dubious morals. All three of them ended up very successful and big fans of the Lord of Hell. His popularity rating on the social hell channels was going up. Especially since he'd rid himself of a media rival. Black holes could be wonderful things.

"Calm your panties, or better yet, drop them and go commando. Weren't you listening when I read the letter? Merry is not asking for a toy. She said, 'help me.'"

"Help her by helping her son."

"Bah. That's your interpretation," he scoffed.

"For a smart devil, you are sometimes woefully stupid," she muttered.

"Would you like to wager, wench of mine?" Lucifer asked with a slow smile. "I swear that I will give Merry and her son exactly what they need. If Merry thanks me for my intervention and hands me her soul voluntarily, you will spend one week bowing to my greatness and massaging my feet."

Gaia's brow arched. "I bow to no one."

"I see, you're afraid of losing. Nice, if a bit gag worthy, of you to admit you're wrong."

"I'm not wrong. You are going to muck up this woman's life. No way she agrees to give you her soul."

"If you're that confidant, then what's the harm in betting?"

Gaia pursed her lips. "Fine. But if you lose, you'll be on diaper duty for a week. No help. At all."

"A week?" He gulped. His children were toxic. Why, just last week Jujube had a shit that melted all the hairs on his body, and he'd been three rooms away!

"Well? Is it a deal, or are you afraid you'll lose?" She knew how to tease him so well.

"Fine," he grumbled, not worried at all. He was putting his best man on the job. One of the few he called friend.

A demon who had no problem saying, "Fuck off, I am not your errand boy," when Lucifer made his demand.

But the devil had been bargaining his whole life. He could see inside of people, and demons, to find the one thing they really craved. A desire they didn't even recognize sometimes. In the end, Lucifer got what he wanted, and his friend got a seemingly good deal.

Gaia remained unimpressed. "I can't believe Marduke agreed to your terms."

"Always know the weaknesses of others to achieve your end goal." Sage words for his listening son.

"I'm not sure I see how your plan is supposed to work."

"That's the beauty of it. It's subtle."

Gaia snorted. "Not really. You've been watching

the Hellmark Channel again with all its romantically demonic holiday movies."

"Have not." A hot denial. Also a lie.

"Really, you're not thinking of setting up a poor single mother with your kennel master?"

"You caught me. So what if I am. I'd be giving them both what they want."

"And what does the boy get out of it?"

"A puppy."

5

No amount of pleading with Miguel could stop his rage, a thing of violence that had probably been brewing all day. Poor baby. All that emotion stuck inside. He needed an outlet.

The moment Merry opened the bin of Christmas stuff and pulled out the plastic Santa, he exploded.

Santa died. As did the rest of the things in the box.

"You work it out, baby. Kill that stuff." She encouraged him to express himself, something the doctor said could prove cathartic. At least it was something other than the apathy she hated so much.

Miguel shouldn't move around so silently and

without expression. A child should be talking and laughing, having fun. Was he enjoying smashing the stuff in the bin?

He certainly went about it methodically.

"Look, baby, you missed a ball." A plastic one that squished flat when stomped.

In the midst of Miguel's emotional expression, a knock arrived at her door. Terrible timing. Her son needed her right now.

She ignored it and so did he to kick at some tinsel.

"That's it, baby. You work out all those nasty emotions." She should have known he might react badly given he'd been getting tense ever since the Christmas-themed items emerged in stores. His dad had died a year ago, killed by a fake Santa with a gun.

A thing like that apparently stuck with a child.

Bang. Bang. Bang. The solid pounding rattled the door loud enough that Miguel paused. They both stared.

The locks, three of them in total, clicked and slid as if opened by a key.

No one but her had the keys. She rose from the floor and gasped as the door opened.

The frame filled with a big man—truly

imposing—with jet-black hair and eyes that glowed green for a second like an animal's caught in a headlight. He wore a calf-length dark gray duster and big boots streaked with dirt and had a stubbled jaw and a scowl.

It might have been a while since she'd been to church, but she made the sign of the cross—at her back—and Miguel gagged.

The big man also grimaced. "Seriously?" He glanced past her and frowned even deeper. "What is going on?"

"Uh." She found herself at a rare loss for words.

The guy snapped his fingers. "Hello. Are you high? Because if you're high, this will have to wait."

"What will have to wait?" Did he speak of her death? She wondered given the size of his hands.

Rather than reply, he dug around inside his coat and retrieved something.

Not a gun.

Something even more surprising, which he cradled in the nook of his arm.

Merry couldn't help but exclaim, "Is that a puppy?"

6

THE WOMAN'S expression lit with excitement.

Marduke's clouded with confusion.

A moment ago, in the hall outside the apartment, it sounded as if a war was going on within. Crashing and banging. He'd almost left when the door opened. Odd given no one stood by it. The lovely woman with the dark hair within appeared surprised to see him.

And way too human.

Which was why he'd argued with Lucifer's demand.

"I need you to bring a puppy to a woman and her brat."

"The only one I have was reserved for you."

Lucifer waved a hand. "I'll wait for the next batch. She needs it now."

"If you say so. Where am I delivering it?"

"Earth."

Marduke blinked. "You want me to drop a hellhound off on Earth?"

"Do you need me to talk slower?" Lucifer rolled his eyes. "Yes, Earth. By the way, they're human, so you'll need to show them how to train their hellhound."

"You're kidding, right?"

The devil proved serious enough he offered Marduke too many tempting prizes in exchange for this favor, the biggest one being a Hell Cruise. Marduke had heard good things about the one through the Bermuda Triangle. And they were pet friendly.

More perks got tossed on as Marduke argued about how a few hours might not be enough to teach humans how to not get eaten by the puppy currently in a chewing phase. In Hell, their kennels were reinforced because their first set of teeth were so fucking sharp.

But the devil always got what he wanted, so here he was, on Earth, presenting a puppy to the dumb human reaching for it and crooning, "Hello there, you cutie-patootie."

He leaned back. "Don't touch the puppy. It will bite."

"That cute little thing would never hurt anyone." She clapped and almost bounced. "Who are you giving it to? It's going to make someone so happy."

"Happy, right." He glanced down at the pup, who trembled and leaned against him. Yeah, she was scaring him, too. He should have asked the devil for more favors. This task might be more complicated than even he predicted. "Are you Merry Garcia?"

"Why yes I am! And you are?"

"Marduke," he answered without thinking. He bit his tongue before he added, the Devil's kennel master. The Dark Lord hadn't mentioned whether or not his position was to be a secret.

"Marmaduke, just like Great Dane in that movie." She sounded so excited.

Indignation filled him. "Mar. Duke. And not a dog." A demon. Another thing left unsaid, although judging by her vapid grinning, she might not have cared.

"How can I help you, Marduke?" The dumb lady beamed at him, ignoring the fact a stranger had walked in who could have strangled her one handed. How had she lived this long?

"I'm here to deliver something to you."

"Really?" Her eyes widened. "From who?"

Lucifer had been very clear on this point when briefing him. "Satan sent it."

"Santa?"

"Satan."

"That's what I said. Santa."

He rolled his eyes. "Whatever. Says to tell you he got your letter, and this is just the start to fulfilling your demands."

"Santa sent you to help. Meaning you must be an elf," she exclaimed. "You're taller than expected. Where's your tassels and bells?"

He blinked. Not something he did often since his eyes didn't give a shit if he lubricated or not. "Do I look like a fucking elf?"

"Language! Tiny ears," she chided, finger wagging. Not a good thing to do in front of a possibly hungry puppy.

"Listen, lady. Fuck is a word like any other. Get over it."

"I don't want Miguel to have a potty mouth."

"Then teach him not to say bad things." Seemed pretty easy to him.

"But that would be stifling his expression. Best if he never learns them in the first place."

He stared at her. "Lady, you are all kinds of special."

"Thank you." She beamed. "So, tell me more about what Santa sent. And before Christmas, too. How absolutely lovely of him especially since I'm sure he's very busy. Thank him for me, please."

Marduke winced, imagining the Dark Lord's reply to that. "Yeah, let's save the thanks. He'd prefer not to have them."

"How noble. I don't suppose you could give him a hug from me, then?"

"No. Let's get to business. This dog is for you." He set the gift on the floor. where it sat at attention, alert, not that you could tell with its floppy ears. Some kind of defect compared to the other hounds and why he'd chosen it for this task.

"Oh, it's just darling."

"Yeah, you might want to hold off on that thought. This here is a special breed of dog."

"I'm sure it is. So cute." She dropped to rub the puppy's head. It craned and gave Marduke a what-the-fuck look.

"It's a trained killer."

"This sweet thing? No way." She kissed its nose

and stood. "But adorable as it is, I'm afraid I can't take the puppy."

"Oh yes you are."

She shook her head. "Our apartment lease specifically states no pets."

"This isn't negotiable. You are keeping the dog and will learn how to control it."

"Control?" She recoiled. "It's a living creature with free will."

"Like the will to tear out your throat," he muttered.

"Excuse me?"

"Nothing. Fuck."

"Language."

He glowered.

She smiled.

Marduke's frown deepened as the young boy approached and put his hand on the dog, then sat beside it and put his whole arm around.

The women's face melted, and a hint of tears brimmed as she looked at him and said, "We're keeping it. What's its name?"

7

Who cared what the lease said? The moment Merry saw how Miguel bonded right away with the dog, she made her decision. She'd move if the landlord had a problem with it.

They went off to the far corner of the living room. Together. And dare she say Miguel looked a bit happier than before?

"The puppy has no official designation. It is up to the owners to decide, as names have power."

"No name? We'll have to think of something. Rufus? Clifford?" She tapped her lower lip. "Hmm. This will take some thought. But where are my manners? Come in." She closed the door behind Marduke, all too aware of how much space he took. How manly he appeared.

Any nervousness at his sudden arrival disappeared at the sight of the puppy. Bad people didn't go around with puppies, unless— She glanced at him and asked, "Do you own a white van?"

"No."

"Excellent." She bustled the two steps to her kitchen and made a platter of crackers and cheese. Both the processed kind. She poured grape juice into plastic tumblers. She carried out her charcuterie spread on a Paw Patrol platter found at the dollar store to the living room. He still stood, looking at the mess on the floor.

"What happened?" He waved a hand to encompass the destruction.

She set the tray down on her reclaimed crate table by the sofa she'd salvaged, the cushions stuffed with clothing that had outlived its purpose. "Having suffered emotional trauma, Miguel found himself needing to physically express his feelings."

"The kid had a tantrum." Marduke glanced from her to Miguel. "You. Kid. Clean up that mess."

Miguel glanced at Marduke but continued to pet the dog.

She intervened. "Not needed."

"He did it. He cleans it."

"No, he doesn't have to. He's had a rough time."

She excused Miguel, but Marduke wouldn't have it.

"Don't make excuses for shit behavior. Time he learns how it works." He focused on Miguel. "You wanna break stuff? You clean it up. That's not up to your mother to do. So get a broom."

Miguel paused.

Marduke kept staring and growled, "Now, boy."

For a second, Miguel's expression tightened, and he stood, bristling puppy by his side. He held Marduke's gaze.

The man won the staring contest. Miguel relaxed before offering a short nod. He then proceeded to clean.

Gaping proved to be the only thing Merry was capable of. She'd never seen Miguel calm so quickly from a rage. And he was tidying. Not something he'd done in the last year. He usually preferred to make messes.

Once Miguel was done, he returned and stood a few paces from Marduke, who nodded. "Good job. Now for some lessons about your puppy. What you've got there is a hellhound."

"I don't think I've heard of that breed," she mused aloud.

"Because they're rare on Earth."

She caught the odd statement. "Where are they native to, then?"

"Hell."

"The place in Norway?"

He stared.

"Or is it Greenland?" She frowned. She knew it wasn't in North America.

"Hellhounds are the top of the canine food chain. They are tough, loyal to their masters, and deadly, too. They require a firm hand at all times."

"Or we'll raise it in love and let it be the puppy it was meant to be," she enthused.

There Marduke went staring at her again. "Are you for real?"

"I am. You?" She reached out and poked him. In the belly. Her finger met a hard slab.

Oh.

Wait, that came out of her mouth. Her startled gaze met his.

He frowned.

A little hand tugged, and she looked down. Miguel pulled her away from Marduke. Shoved her to the sofa then turned to glare at the big man.

"You're a tad small yet to challenge me, little man. But tell you what, treat the hound right, and you won't have anyone that will ever bother you, no matter what your size." Marduke uttered a sharp whistle, and the puppy bolted for him and skidded to a stop by his feet.

Miguel's eyes widened.

"Ready to learn what your dog can do?"

At Miguel's rapid nod, Marduke showed them the basic commands using hand signals. Up. Down. Rollover. Attack. Menace. Protect.

Merry had no problem with any of them, and then added one of her own at the end. She jazzed her fingers and said, "Dance."

"A hellhound doesn't dance."

"It just needs to be taught. I once knew this girl who had a dog that would dance on its hind legs for treats." Cutest thing ever. Maybe she could find a tutu and make a video for Miguel.

"If a hellhound is hungry, it will just eat the nearest person. Which could be its master, so always have lots of food on hand. Raw meat being the best, although they do enjoy a nice beefsicle."

"I guess it's a good thing we're not vegan, then." Miguel functioned better on high protein. "You haven't said if it's a boy or girl."

Marduke shrugged. "Because it hasn't decided yet."

She blinked. "I didn't know that was a thing."

"Now you do."

'And when will it happen?"

"When it's ready." The man revealed as little as possible.

Miguel moved off and practiced the hand gestures. The dog obeyed without fail.

"How often does it eat?" she asked.

"As often as it likes."

A non-answer. "And potty breaks?"

Marduke shrugged. "In the kennels, they go at will. Show it the exits and it should figure it out."

She glanced at the doorknob then the dog shaking paws with Miguel. "I'll need a collar and leash."

"I brought a set, actually." The man pulled them from his coat, a big chain thing that clinked horribly and a short sturdy rope to latch on.

"Those won't do. But I think I have something." A filmy pink scarf that tied in a perfect bow and the extendible clothesline she kept in her shower. "Tada!" She beamed.

Marduke's face appeared as if he might be constipated. Hopefully, the juice he chugged would do its charm.

"This is emasculating for us all," Marduke declared.

"I think it's cute. I'm going to take it for a walk. Coming, Miguel?"

Her son bolted to get his boots and coat. The enthusiasm made her smile. She glanced at Marduke, a man who probably had better things to do, and yet, she couldn't help a lilting query, "Coming?"

8

Coming?

Marduke might if she kept looking at him that way. Crazy lady was cute as fuck. Also nuts. She treated him and the hellhound as if they were tame.

Far from it. Yet there was a certain perverse novelty in following along. She babbled incessantly all the way down the stairs. The boy never replied. Neither did Marduke. It didn't seem to bother her.

She hit the slushy sidewalk, ignored the biting cold, and walked the damned dog, who behaved even as it cast woebegone glances at him.

Sorry, buddy. He was just doing the devil's work.

Christmas lights shone in windows and on the skinny poles lining the sidewalks. City living meant tolerating crowded spaces. Kind of like Hell. Which was why Marduke spent most of his time in the kennels. People were overrated.

The boy hunched in his coat, his gaze on the dog and nothing else. Marduke couldn't blame him. It appeared as if Christmas had puked all over town.

As Merry skipped ahead, the smell of brimstone preceded the arrival of the Dark Lord.

"What the fuck do you want?" Marduke muttered, glancing ahead at Merry, who seemed oblivious that the devil had joined them. Miguel held the makeshift leash with her and also didn't peek.

"They can't see us," Lucifer advised. "Good job on delivering the puppy."

"Exactly what the fuck are you plotting? Or is it your plan to have her mauled to death?"

"That won't happen if you stick around long enough to ensure everything goes okay."

"How long?"

"Depends on how quickly things progress. What do you think about her?"

"She's—" A bunch of words came to mind, but it was Lucifer's grin that triggered Marduke's epiphany. "You're trying to set me up!"

"Me?" False innocence from the man wearing red and green so bright Marduke's eyes hurt.

"I'm telling you right now I am not banging her."

"Would you prefer to make love? She seems the type," Lucifer mused aloud. "Annoying at first, until you realize love equals swallow."

"I am not looking for a relationship."

"Your lips say that, but your heart…" Lucifer sighed. "It really needs a bypass."

"My heart is fine. And so is my life."

"Your life sucks."

"Says the man who smells of baby shit."

Lucifer glanced down at his feet. "Gaia warned me about feeding Jujube hellapeno poppers. Next time I'll stick to beans, the magical fruit."

"Why are you here? I'm doing as you asked. I delivered the puppy. They're learning to handle it and will probably be eaten, I predict, by the end of the week."

"No, they won't. You underestimate Merry and Miguel. Especially the boy."

"The kid." Marduke snorted, and at that moment, Miguel turned to look right at him. Then the devil. The child stared right at him, and Lucifer waved in reply. Miguel nodded before paying attention to the hound once more.

"He can see you."

"The boy and I are already acquainted because of his father. I predict he'll have a long and sinful future. If he survives childhood."

The screeching of tires had Merry turning too slow to see the car as it sped past, one window down, the muzzle of a gun poking from it.

And what did the fool woman do?

Threw herself over the dog and her kid, singing loudly.

9

"Fa-la-la-la!" Merry sang at the top of her lungs to counter the crackle of gunfire while she covered puppy and Miguel, with no thought other than that of a mother to protect. The expected bullets never hit because suddenly, there was another body on top, a big one with a large coat that fell on either side like a drape.

The moment lasted an eternity of a second before a gruff Marduke declared, "They're gone."

"They'll be back," she chirped.

"What makes you say that?" He glanced down at her. "Do you know them?"

"Not exactly." She handed the leash to Marduke before she scooped Miguel into her arms. He was getting too big to carry, and yet she needed to hug him. She whispered against his ear, "It's okay, baby. Mama's here. You're okay."

The same words she'd said the night he saw his father shot by Santa. A case of Brian in an alley at the wrong time. A robbery gone wrong the cops claimed.

It should have ended there, only it appeared Santa had a lot of cash and drugs on him when he died in a hail of gunfire. Also in front of Miguel.

The cops took it into custody, meaning the gang relying on it didn't get paid. And they blamed Merry.

She'd moved to get away from them, only it appeared they'd found her. But what would killing her accomplish?

Marduke kept pace with her and grumbled, "Why are you being shot at?"

"Because of a misunderstanding. Unfortunately, they've yet to listen."

"So they're trying to kill you?" Marduke scooped up the puppy and then eyed her carrying Miguel, who sucked on his thumb.

Uh-oh.

"Hand him over."

"It's okay. I've got him. Besides, I think the puppy is heavier."

"I can carry both," he grumbled, tucking the dog back into an inner pocket. He then reached again.

She wanted to huff that she could do it, but Miguel was stiff as a board and a lot heavier at this age than was easy to carry.

"Baby," she murmured. "Can Marduke carry you so we can walk faster?" She wanted to be far away before the cops arrived with their many questions.

Miguel turned his head. He and Marduke exchanged a glance that saw her boy leaving her arms. A relief because she could now walk better, but guilt filled her, too. As if she'd failed.

Their pace quickened, but that didn't stop Marduke from suddenly turning loquacious. "You weren't surprised by the attack. Why?"

"Because bad people don't give up. We should go." She needed to get home and pack for a stealthy move. The third one since last Christmas. Santa must have known she'd be between homes. Hence why he sent the puppy early!

The jolly man truly was all knowing.

"What's happening to you, pita? Who are those pricks?"

"No one you need to worry about." She wondered why he called her a breaded pocket.

"Never said I was worried. More like curious about the cowards. In my day, we fought face to face."

Judging by his slightly crooked nose, he told the truth. "At your size, I'm sure fighting is a great answer, but I have Miguel to think of. I won't have him in harm's way. Now ixnay on the shooters."

"Ix what?"

"It means shut it. Miguel doesn't need to hear it."

"He didn't. I muted our conversation."

The most inane thing for him to say. He obviously wasn't a parent. Kids heard everything.

"The shooting wasn't random. You're in danger."

"Everyone is in danger from the moment they're conceived. Life is hard. We just have to keep on chugging along best we can," she enthused.

"Are you always this full of shit? It's like you're determined to be deliberately obtuse when it comes to reality."

"More like I won't give in to the negativity. Life is as hard as we make it. I am choosing to enjoy mine."

"You'd enjoy more if you punched something I'll bet."

Remembering her earlier poke into rock, she didn't hit him. "I'll take Miguel and the puppy back now. We're almost there. It's been lovely meeting you. Thanks for the dog. Really appreciate it."

"Fucker, you did this on purpose!" Marduke glared at the ground as if speaking to someone before grumbling, "I am not leaving you until I know you're secure."

"You don't have to do that."

"Not for you. For the pup. I won't have it in harm's way." He glowered in her direction.

"Of course, you wouldn't," she agreed softly, wondering if he knew how at odds his gruff words and expression were with his actions thus far. Look how Miguel relaxed in the big man's grip. "We're fine. But you can spend the night if it makes you feel better. The couch is a great napping spot."

"I don't sleep on couches."

"We could give you blankets for the floor."

The corner of his lip twitched slightly as he drawled, "Not gonna offer me your bed? That would be the charitable thing to do."

"If you had nowhere to go, but if you stay, that's your choice and that means I keep my bed because you, of course, are a gentleman who would never think of kicking me out." She batted her lashes for good measure.

Marduke pinched the bridge of his nose. "Lady, you are giving me a headache."

"You should try yoga. It's great. Although it can get smelly if you're too relaxed." Her nose wrinkled.

He stared at her.

"What?"

"The strangest things come out of your mouth."

"They're called words."

"You have too many of them," he complained.

"You can leave anytime."

"I will if you tell me who those guys were that were shooting at you."

"Guys? That's a sexist assumption."

"It's a generalized expression. You know what I mean." He grimaced. He really was too cute playing angry all the time.

"Even if I knew the names of the people in that car, it wouldn't matter. They're only the tip of the gang in this city."

"So move."

"Easy to say. I need a job to rent a place, and that's harder in smaller places," she muttered. Left unmentioned, the help she needed for Miguel didn't extend much past the city limits. And she didn't have a car, a must for even suburban living.

As they neared the corner to turn onto her block, she heard the sirens and a whiff of the air held smoke. Amidst the clamor of approaching fire engines, her steps slowed to a stop on the sidewalk. She watched as the apartment building burned. A total loss for her apartment at least, judging by the window with shooting flames.

Looking on the bright side, she'd been meaning to move them to a nicer neighborhood. This would be a positive thing. Start over fresh. New place. New things. Same life…

Someone in the gathering crowd began to sing off-key, "Siren night, smoky night, all is chaos, fire so bright. Round the burning building, mother and child. Holy hot firemen, tender and fine." Then they switched abruptly to, "We wish you a merry Christmas, and a fiery new year. Praise Satan!"

Miguel shoved to be let down and watched, with jaw dropped, the inferno versus the firemen. To her surprise, Marduke remained by her side while the fire was fought and contained.

He said nothing until she scooped a sleepy-eyed little boy into her arms. "Time to get you to bed," she whispered, placing a kiss on Miguel.

"Where are you going to stay? Do you need to go to a motel?"

"We'll find our own way. You can go. I've got this." A lie, but her issues weren't his problem.

"It's winter and minus too fucking much," he pointed out. "Do you have someone you can call?"

She shook her head. Orphaned at seventeen, she'd been working too many jobs in order to survive to make any friends. "Miguel is my only family."

"What about his daddy? Could you stay with him?"

"I guess we could."

Marduke accompanied her in the taxi, and it was only as it pulled up outside a cemetery that he growled, "What kind of joke is this?"

"This is where Miguel's daddy lives now." Not in the consecrated part or they wouldn't be able to visit often. "There's a nice tree by his grave. A good wind break, with sheltering boughs."

"Sleeping outside in winter is dangerous."

"God will watch over us."

"God had a mental break and is on a sabbatical. You're on your own."

"I'm sure we'll land on our feet." She clung tight to her optimism. It was all she had left other than her son.

"Lucifer is going to pay large for this," Marduke muttered before snapping, "Driver, take us to a nice motel." Then added, "It better be dog friendly."

10

FINDING A MOTEL PROVED EASY. Marduke used his Hellcard—good in all the nine circles and anywhere fraud was accepted—to pay for it. The attendant paid them little mind, not looking up from his phone as he handed over two keys.

The motel was the kind with a wing on either side of the office. Their rooms were on the first level, side by side with a cheater door between them.

"This is yours." Marduke handed over a key and shoved Merry in the direction of number twelve. The boy clutched her hand.

"Thank you. This is really nice of you to help us." It should have been sarcastic, not sincere.

The boy eyed him and inclined his head, his

version of thanks. The puppy didn't glance his way at all, following at his little master's heels. The leash still in Marduke's hand.

It wouldn't be needed. The dog and boy were already bonding. Which was good.

The bad being, what the fuck had he gotten himself into? Why was he still on Earth? He should be back in Hell. But no, someone had to go and shoot at them and now he was in a shitty motel.

"Lucifer!" He only had to say it once.

"Marduke. My good friend." The devil appeared in a new outfit—one that smelled less like shit—with Junior by his side. A mini-me in matching red jogging suit, bedazzled gold, and wearing shades.

"What the fuck is going on?" Marduke really didn't care about rank. Not after all this time.

"I'd like to know the same thing. Here you are at a sleazy motel. Alone. Where the fuck is Merry?" the devil chastised.

"She's in the next room because someone set her building on fire."

"Well, that's a stroke of bad luck. Good thing you're sticking around for a bit to help her out."

Marduke glowered. "No, I'm not."

"Are you reneging? Because I believe our deal

was that you can't leave until Merry and son are settled with the dog."

"Dog is with them."

"But they're not settled, so better get cracking before I lose the bet with my wife."

"I don't give a flying fuck about your bet. I want to know what the deal is with Merry." He pointed to the adjoining door.

"She wrote me a lovely letter."

"Asking for a dog?" Because that part wasn't clear.

"Not exactly."

"I'm assuming you thought the dog would protect her, but it's still young. And she's got some trigger-happy asshats coming after her."

"And?"

"What are you gonna do about it?"

"Nothing because that would be interfering in mortal affairs."

"Since when has that stopped you?"

"You're right, it doesn't, which is why you're here."

Marduke crossed his arms. "I'm not a soldier. I can't protect her."

"I'd say you showed fine instincts on that sidewalk."

"I have duties to attend. I can't stick around as a bodyguard." Even if the idea intrigued. He'd felt something when he'd thrown himself over her and the young'uns. A twinge in his black heart.

"Then don't stay. Go ahead. Leave."

Marduke got a foreboding feeling. "What are you up to, you old goat?"

"Me? Nothing," the devil lied grandly.

"Whatever it is, do not get me involved. I have no interest in your shenanigans. Nor do I have time to waste. You know Morgana is due to litter any day now."

"I know. Don't forget you promised me one." The devil glanced down at his son, who was toddling for the booze bar. "Bring us both a beer, would ya?"

The boy giggled. Still adorable. But Lucifer had a bad feeling about the child. Better not get too attached.

"I'll give you two if I can leave." As kennel master, he carefully controlled supply and owners. It was part of his contract.

"Two? Now that's tempting. Done. Deal. You may leave."

Marduke had won. He glanced at the adjoining door. "What about Merry and Miguel?"

"Apparently not your problem."

"Are you going to get someone to guard them?"

"It's almost Christmas. Do you know how hard it is to find someone who hasn't made some desperate plans in an attempt to pretend they actually have a meaningful existence?"

"Um, not many?"

"You. I had you. And you would rather go back your dogs. So shoo. Vamoose."

"What about Merry?"

"She'll probably die and end up in my court before New Year's."

The very idea had him uttering a stark, "No. I can't let that happen."

"Stop with all that caring, right now, mister. I will puke."

"I don't care."

"If you say so. Not that it matters. Her soul will soon reside in Hell."

"What of the boy?"

"Hell, too."

The idea they'd both die bothered. "I won't let that happen."

"Look at you caring again. Gag."

A glower went with Marduke's muttered, "No, I don't."

"Whatever. Stay. Go. I don't care. I'm leaving the decision up to you."

"Me?"

"You're a strong, capable man. I'm sure you'll do the wrong thing. Come, Junior. Let's go toss condoms full of glitter on those miserable suits working Wall Street."

The devil left.

Marduke went to call a portal but stopped. Should he say goodbye? He'd rather not, as that could easily get messy. Leaving without a word, though, seemed slimier.

With a heavy sigh, he opened the adjoining door and beckoned Merry. She sat in a chair watching over Miguel, who lay under the covers, the dog draped over his feet.

She kissed the boy's forehead before silently joining him. She closed the door most of the way before saying, "Thanks for the room. I'll be sure to pay you back the cost once we get settled."

"I don't fucking care about the price. Stay as long as you need. Think of it as another present."

He couldn't hide from the blooming rainbow of happiness that transformed her face.

"Thank you!" She sounded genuinely grateful. Perhaps this wouldn't be so bad.

"I have to go."

"Okay."

"As in leave. Forever," he reiterated in case it wasn't clear.

"Of course, you do. Busy man like yourself." She grabbed his hand and uttered with earnest fervor, "Thanks for your help, Marduke. God bless you and Merry Christmas."

11

She'd not only used the other lord's name, she'd also named the day that should not be named. Marduke winced.

She apologized. "Was it something I said? Oh my, are you Jewish? Happy Hanukah. Or do you celebrate Kwanzaa?"

"Don't thank me. And don't use the G word."

"God?"

He grimaced.

She cocked her head and did the sign of the cross, which had him baring his teeth.

"Oh." She laughed. "So funny. Do you often pretend to be a vampire? I thought those were usually clean shaven and wearing ruffled shirts."

Did she really think to compare him to that pathetic version? "I am not a vampire."

"You're right. Not pale enough," she mused aloud. "And everyone knows Satanists wear suits and work in office buildings." She grinned impishly.

It was cute even as it made him wonder. "Do you ever take anything seriously?"

For a second her mien sobered. "Rarely, because when I do, I get sad." Her lips turned down.

He didn't like it one bit. "Don't you dare cry."

"I won't. I learned crying doesn't fix anything. Neither does a bad attitude."

"A bad attitude keeps annoying folk away," he grumbled.

"Are you sure? Because I'm still here." She winked and laughed.

Despite himself, he almost smiled. "Listen, I'm serious about having to go."

"Don't apologize. You've already done so much, and you are surely a busy man."

"You're not upset?" he questioned. Most women tended to cling. And the more they clung, the more he wanted to give them a shove. Only he didn't push women, so instead, he glowered and didn't let them get close in the first place. Merry, though, appeared to ignore all his cues.

"Upset?" Her lips tilted. "Never. After all, this isn't goodbye but until the next time!"

Being a dick, he usually would have indicated there would be no next time. Only he found himself oddly hesitating. "Are you sure you'll be okay?" He could have kicked himself for asking. Now that he'd opened that door, she'd make some excuse about why he had to stay and, when he said no, would either resort to tears or guilt him into remaining.

"I'll be fine. Don't worry about me." She actually began moving him for the door.

He should have been fine with it, but something didn't feel right. He felt oddly…responsible? It made no sense. He'd done what he'd come to do. He owed her nothing more. Still, he dug into his pocket and handed her a piece of plastic. "Here's my credit card. Use it to order whatever you need."

"So generous, but I couldn't." She tucked her hands behind her back.

"Don't be too proud."

"Not pride, merely aware I could never repay you for your kindness already."

Damn her for being so irritatingly polite. He growled. "Never said you had to."

She stared at him. Intent. Studying. Before saying, "Why?" Just one word yet it hit him like a fist to the gut.

Why was he acting so out of character? What was it about her? "Why? Because I just gave you a puppy and I'll be pissed if you both end up dead because you had to spend the night on the streets. If you don't give a shit about yourself, think about the boy and the dog." A low blow, and he saw the pinching of her features for a moment before her plastic smile returned.

"You're right. I should be thinking of others. My pride is getting in the way." She tucked the card into a pocket before rolling her shoulders. With a shyer demeanor than usual, she said, "Surely there must be something I can do in return."

He didn't know what possessed him to say it. But he did.

"If you want to pay me, then a kiss."

12

THERE WAS a name for women who traded kisses for stuff, but Merry ignored that as she digested his odd request. Or maybe not so strange given there was a vibe between them. She found him extremely attractive, and while he was gruff, she'd noticed his respect toward her.

And now he asked for a kiss?

She should have specified it would be just one, no tongue, or stood up for herself and told him where to go. But this scowling hunk of a man wanted to kiss her.

She was feminine and vain enough to want to see if it would be any good. She uttered an enthusiastic, "Okay," and flung her arms around his neck. Mashed her mouth on his, and swooned.

Best. Kiss. Ever.

It should be noted Merry hadn't been with a lot of men. Three in her whole life. The last one being Miguel's daddy. She'd never been wowed before.

Because this embrace was definitely giving her hot tingles all over.

At first, he was stiff, his body tense even as his lips parted on a surprised gasp. His paralysis didn't last long before his arms wrapped around her and he literally lifted her off her feet.

There was something to be said for a big and burly man. She felt delicate in his grip. He held her firmly, but oh so gently. His embrace was soft, and she could tell he held back.

"I'm not going to break."

The kiss turned into something hot and breathy, with tongue and moaning, mostly by her. Her legs ended up wrapped around him, and she would have gladly kept riding him if he'd not been a gentleman.

He tore his mouth away and grumbled, "I didn't give you my card so you'd have sex with me."

It took effort to open her passion-heavy lids and drawl, "The sex we're going to have is because I am ridiculously attracted to you."

He went stiff. All over. And he didn't melt. Not yet.

"You do realize I can't offer you anything permanent. One night, that's it."

"Anyone ever tell you that you talk too much?" She silenced him with a kiss, knowing she was acting even crazier than usual, but after the strife of the last year, she needed relief. Pleasure.

To feel something other than the forced happiness to hide the stress and anxiety.

She plastered herself against him, her fingers clutching at his broad shoulders, practically climbing him in her eagerness. He held her, his hands grabbing her ass and giving her a boost to reach that yummy mouth of his.

The passion wasn't one sided.

He kissed her, his lips hard and commanding, but at the same time gentle. Coaxing her mouth to open that his tongue might tease. But soon all the hot embraces couldn't stop the raging desire.

She whispered against his mouth, "Let's get rid of these clothes."

He groaned. "This is such a bad idea."

"Would you like to stop?" She had to respect his wishes after all.

His eyes blazed, the darkness of them almost

glowing orange. Holy smokes. Was she glimpsing his passion? How sexy.

"I want you," was all he replied. His fingers were deft as he stripped them both because she got distracted by the hard planes of his body. Her hands skimmed over his flesh, knotted with muscles, but also some scars.

"What happened to you?"

"Work hazard," he murmured, finishing the removal of her clothes. Down on his haunches by her feet, he stared up at her.

She was so damned wet, and she would have sworn he knew it in the way he purred, "Delicious."

He rose, inches and inches of man. Naked. His shaft jutting. Oh, the size.

She only got a glimpse before he bracketed her with his arms and had her back against a wall. His thigh pushed at the seam of her legs, and she parted them. He inserted himself and pressed against her. She gasped as she ground his thigh against her. His mouth caught her panting breath.

While they kissed, she touched him all over. Wide shoulders. Bulging arms. Thick chest.

His hands slid down her body, skimming over her back to her waist, then her hips, and finally he gripped her thighs. She lifted one leg and wrapped it around his waist in invitation. He got the hint. He wedged a hand between their bodies, cupping her mound before dipping a finger.

He stroked her, and she moaned in soft pleasure. Panted as he rubbed her, faster and faster. Then he stopped the friction against her clit to slip his finger into her ready sex.

She clamped down hard on it, and it was his turn to groan. "Fuck me, I need a taste."

He dropped to his knees, and he showed her heaven was a real place as he licked her so good she came so hard she found herself fisting his hair. "Sorry."

"Don't be," he growled before lavishing her pussy with more attention until she bucked and writhed, whimpering for relief.

He stood, and with eyes heavy with desire, she gazed down to see his massive cock. Long. Thick. Desiring her.

"Yes." She didn't even realize she hissed it aloud until he lifted her, his hands palming her ass, while she braced herself against his shoulders.

The head of his cock nudged, and she shuddered.

He froze. "Merry?"

Did he really think he needed to ask? Her legs wound tighter around his waist.

"Now, Duke," she murmured.

He slid slowly into her, the length of him, the girth, a sensual tease. Her pussy squeezed him as he seated himself deep. So deep, and she could feel his shaft pulsing.

Too late she thought about a condom. But at least she was on the pill. Because no way was she letting him pull out as he started to move.

It felt so good. He started with a grinding that had her digging in her nails and gasping. Then short thrusts, which made her squeak.

And then she couldn't think or speak at all as pleasure enveloped her. His cock hit a sweet spot inside of her that made her gasp. She came again, his mouth catching her climax cry, his body shuddering as he found release in her.

He stilled, buried deep. His lips clung to hers.

Still, she managed to whisper, "Wow."

He managed a rusty chuckle. "No shit, wow. Sorry I was in a rush. Next time, I'll take it slower."

Next time?

Happened in bed and it was possibly better. She might need him to try again to be sure. She washed up after. Actually, he bathed her with a warm cloth, his touch gentle, before he carried her back to bed. His bed.

"Miguel," she protested.

"Is fine. Door's open. Dog's with him. Let's go to bed."

She chose not to argue with the guy who'd made her see heaven.

Turned out the big man was a spooner. And she had the best night's sleep until the rude awakening the next morning.

13

"What the fuck!" Marduke bellowed as the blankets got wet, very wet. Because a certain little boy was pissing on his side.

"Miguel. No." His mother scrambled upright. "This isn't the potty, baby."

The boy knew it and finished his tinkle with a shake.

"That little shit did it on purpose." Just a like a dog, marking his territory. In this case, laying claim to his mother. Whom Marduke had defiled. He felt pretty good about that part.

"Don't you yell at him," she chided. "He was obviously disoriented, new place and all. Probably got scared and, rather than look for a potty, he came to find me. It was an accident."

"Accident my ass." He eyed the boy. "Unacceptable. Clean it before I return." The boy might not like finding his mother in bed with Marduke, but that didn't mean he could blatantly disrespect.

Marduke stalked to the bathroom naked, because body shame was an angelic thing. He showered, torn between annoyance at the rude awakening and pleasure. Had last night truly happened?

Merry had kissed him, and it was as if neither of them could resist. The sex had been beyond good. Her enthusiasm, her soft cries, the taste of her...

He flipped back to Hell rather than tug one off. He didn't have time to be decorating the shower tile. He hit his closet for some clothes before he returned, stepping out of the bathroom, only to frown. While his bed had been stripped and changed, Merry and the boy smelled of smoke and piss because their clothing needed a wash. They didn't have a spare set because they'd lost their home.

The reminder wiped his good mood.

"I'll be back. Don't go anywhere," he barked.

He exited the motel and aimed for the nearest discount clothing store a few blocks away, according to the motel attendant. He didn't go alone.

Brimstone barely tickled his nose before Lucifer cleared his throat. "Good morning. Surprised to see you still up here. What happened to leaving?"

Marduke hunched his shoulders. "Something came up."

"Like your dick. I have to say, I am impressed by the speed of your seduction."

It was pretty impressive, and a part of him wanted to beat his chest in masculine pride. He scowled instead. "Fuck off. Not talking about it." He stomped down the sidewalk, his glower clearing people from his path.

"No need to blush. I know it's been a long time for you. I hope you didn't disappoint."

That brought heat to his face. "Would you stop it already? I am not talking about it."

"If you want, I'll over share first. Last night, I took Gaia to dinner. Al fresco on the beach. We had oysters under the moon. And then I pounded her doggie style." The devil mimed holding some hips and thrusting.

"With that kind of spastic technique, I'm

surprised you think yourself qualified to give anyone advice."

Lucifer laughed. "As if I'd show you my true skills. A devil must keep his title as the universe's greatest lover."

"You can keep your skills. I'm doing just fine."

"More than fine, I'd say. I haven't seen you in such a good mood in a long time."

Marduke would have argued, and yet, he did feel rather good. But he wasn't about to give the Dark Lord the smug satisfaction, especially knowing his plan. Which was always doomed to fail.

He wasn't getting into any kind of relationship. Not with a human. And most especially not with Merry. "I'm leaving the second I get them outfitted. They lost all their shit in the fire."

"How kind and generous of you." Lucifer made a moue of displeasure.

"Not really. It's your treasury money."

"What?"

"You told me to use the company card as I saw fit." Yes, he smiled at the way he used his boss's words against him.

"Of all my minions, I didn't expect you to abuse

the privilege." Lucifer grinned. "Way to go! I knew you had it in you."

Marduke only barely resisted rolling his eyes. "Was there an actual reason for your visit this morning?"

"Well, I was thinking. Given it's not safe for Merry and Miguel, maybe she should spend a little bit of time somewhere else. A place the gang-bangers can't touch her."

"Where?" he asked, entering the clothing store and almost marching right back out. He hated shopping. Why hadn't he just let Merry go with the card? "Do you have a spot in mind?"

"You know what they say, there's no place like home for the holidays."

"She has no home."

"I should have said future home. Because where do souls go when they die?" Not to Heaven. Hard to pass the gates before while God was in charge. Now that the angels had taken over, they'd closed the door to all.

"You want me to take her to Hell?" he asked in puzzlement. "But she's not dead."

"Yet." Lucifer eyed his watch.

Marduke grabbed the nearest clothing off racks

and dumped them on a cashier. "You're obviously trying to tell me something, so spit it out."

"Spitting is for vegans who won't swallow a man's swimmers. I'm the great and mighty Lucifer."

"With the worst riddles. Speak plain, for fuck's sake. If you know something that I should, then tell me, or go and annoy someone else," Marduke snapped, losing patience.

"You want the truth? In this case, I'll make an exception." The devil grinned. "You leave and those thugs are coming back. Even if she manages to escape once, they'll find her because the girl won't leave the city."

"Why not?" he exclaimed, exiting the store, not caring at the odd looks he got.

"Because of Miguel's special program for his anger management."

"He just needs a firmer hand," Marduke muttered.

"Well, he'll get one once child services gets a hold him. If he doesn't die when his mother does."

"You make it sound as if it's imminent," he declared, his steps brisk.

Lucifer didn't reply. He didn't have to because

the same car that had shot at Merry the night before went tearing past.

"Fuckers!" Marduke ran and heard a few pops, a scream, but mostly snarls. He arrived in time to find the car parked at a slant, bodies half pulled from the car. Dead. Bleeding.

The hellhound licking its chops.

Miguel, wearing some of that blood, sat beside it with his arm around its neck while Merry stood shell shocked in the door of the motel.

"Merry. You okay?"

Her lips trembled. "No. This is terrible."

"You didn't do anything wrong. The dog just protected and a good thing, too. They would have killed you."

"I know. They'll blame the puppy." She blinked at him before saying, "You have to help me hide it before animal control has it put down."

14

MERRY MIGHT BE in shock at the sudden violence that had occurred, but she remained coherent enough to know that the law would demand her sweet protective puppy be put down. Never mind the dog had saved their lives. Never mind Miguel had already bonded to it.

Faceless bureaucrats would interfere and make her son unhappy. Which, in turn, would make her sad, leaving her with only one choice. She had to ensure no one hurt the puppy-with-no-name.

"You're worried about the fucking dog?" Duke's eyebrows hit new heights.

"You know they'll misinterpret what happened."

"Yeah. I know. Fuck." Marduke rubbed his face.

"I think this time we need to leave the city for good."

"You'll need more than that," he muttered as sirens faintly wailed in the distance.

"I think someone called the police, "she stated as she noticed faces peering between curtains from the motel windows.

"This is bad. And not just for the dog. If someone says you sicced the dog on them, you could be in trouble, too."

She bit her lower lip. "I'll tell them the truth."

"You're not that naïve."

No, she wasn't. Her shoulders slumped. "Guess I'm screwed. But no need for you to get screwed, too. Just promise you'll take the puppy before you go."

"Wait a second. Are you trying to save me?"

"No point in us both going to jail. I don't suppose you'd take Miguel, too? He won't fare well in the foster system."

Her sad face was what did it.

"You're not going to jail."

"We don't have time to escape." Indeed, the first flashing cruiser appeared at the end of the street.

"Trust me." He did appear capable as he first scooped the dog and shoved it back into a pocket, then Miguel with a murmured, "Hold on tight, little man." He then slung an arm around her and said, "Might want to close your eyes for the next part."

Was he expecting them to be shot in a hail of bullets? She tucked her face against him, glad now that she'd taken a chance in his arms the previous night. What a shame it had to end this way.

The sirens faded, replaced by a vast silence that came with cold. So cold she gasped and drew some into her lungs and then couldn't expel it. She could distantly feel his arm around her. A rushing whoosh that turned into a distant mournful scream then a pop as the cold vanished, replaced by heat.

She choked as she expelled the chill from her lungs and took a few heaving breaths that singed before she looked around.

Then she looked again.

Bye-bye, sidewalk outside the motel.

She'd gone from winter in the city to a dusty cobbled road and a cloudy, orange-hued sky, raining ash.

"Where are we?" she asked.

"Welcome to Hell."

She startled at the new voice. Marduke tightened his hold even as he turned them to greet the speaker, a man in his forties, maybe older, with silver temples, distinguished features, wearing a tuxedo. He carried a baby dressed in a frilly red dress, wearing a headband with a massive bow.

"Who are you?" Merry exclaimed.

"I am the one and only amazing Lucifer." He yelped and proffered the baby. "This is the equally wonderful Jujube. And let me repeat, welcome to Hell. My Hell," he purred softly.

"I'm dreaming."

"I assure you you're not. You are indeed in Hell. The first circle, to be exact, because I like to have the kennels near the palace."

She blinked. "Um." She glanced around the reddish hellscape. The smiling man. The scowling Marduke. And finally, her son, who seemed nonplussed that the puppy by his side suddenly had eyes of pure molten red.

She fainted.

15

"What is wrong with you?" Marduke glared at Lucifer. This only after he caught Merry and laid her gently on the ground. Then yelled at the devil.

"Me? I merely thought to greet her, and how does she thank me? Goes to sleep. Rude. I tell you, I'm liking her more and more."

Jujube squirmed and got seated on the ground, where she crawled for the puppy—no wait, the boy—who eyed her with trepidation.

"It's my fault. I didn't warn her we were coming here."

"More like she couldn't handle me in person. It's hard I tell you. People meet me and just can't handle my virility." Lucifer preened.

Marduke sighed. "Why me?" He'd gone long

periods of time without speaking to the Dark Lord, and now he couldn't turn around without running into him.

"Why because it's your turn." Lucifer grinned in a way that boded well for no one.

"Turn for what?"

The devil flicked him a business card. On it a grim reaper scythed a heart with the words, "Grim Dating is dying to match you."

"Oh, like fuck. I told you not to interfere."

"Like I'd listen to you," Lucifer scoffed. "Besides it's too late."

A plaintive mewl drew their attention to Jujube. She wore a pouting lower lip that jutted further when she reached for Miguel, who leaned away, avoiding her touch.

"Looks like my princess is angling for another conquest."

"They're children."

"Until they're not and they're trying to take over the world. At what age do you think generals start amassing their armies?"

"Leave the boy alone."

"That's not up to me." Lucifer snorted. "My girl is like her father. We take. We don't ask. Right, my sugary hellion?"

"Mine." Jujube bounced on her diapered butt and clapped her hands.

Miguel's lips flattened. He didn't appear in agreement. He hugged the dog tighter.

"The boy should be nice to my girl. She's going places. Yes, she is," the devil cooed. "She might even be the one."

"The one to what?" he stupidly asked.

"Read a prophecy and you'll find out. I have. I've read them all." Lucifer giggled, and for a second, the slick devil he knew disappeared and a mad man peered back.

"Can we get back on topic? Now that Merry's in Hell, what's the plan for her and the kid?"

"Glad you asked." Lucifer tucked his hands behind his back. "Given a live soul shouldn't be mixing with damned ones, she'll stay with you in the Kennel Compound."

"What?" It had been a while since he'd had anyone living with him.

"You have lots of room. The dogs will protect them, and you'll be able to continue giving them lessons on their new pet. Win. Win."

"I don't want them here," he snapped, only too late realizing the boy listened.

Miguel's lower lip trembled, and then he bolted.

"Fuck!"

He wasn't the only one peeved. Jujube began to sob. "Mine. Gone."

"Don't worry, sugar butt, Marduke will find him. Let's go see if Cook has some cookies."

"Cookies!" She clapped.

Marduke might have had a hard time tracking one slick-footed little boy but for the bond he had with all his hounds, including the recently gifted puppy. That tie that hadn't fully severed yet but was growing fainter by the moment. It led him to a nearby alley.

Even if it hadn't, he would have heard the snarls. As he entered, those menacing the child backed off. A hellrat, two imps, and a demon that should know better. The hound remained, a guardian to the boy.

Marduke approached slowly, knowing the child would be skittish. There was a time for harsh and a time for soft. He crouched. "You shouldn't run off on your own, little man."

The boy solemnly stared at him.

"It's dangerous."

The boy rolled his eyes and glanced upward.

"Yeah, dangerous there, too, I guess. I take it you ran 'cause you heard me saying I didn't want you staying with me."

The boy offered a small shrug.

"It's not you. It's me." It really was. "I'm an ornery bastard at the best of times. My life is my work. Which is to say the hounds. I don't really have time or the right kind of place for a kid or his mom."

The boy slumped.

And Marduke felt like a shithead. Never mind he owed the kid nothing. It didn't sit well to have him upset. "Guess maybe, though, it wouldn't hurt if you stayed for a night or two."

The kid shifted.

"But you'd be expected to help out with the dogs. You ain't leeching off me."

The boy nodded.

"All right then, we better get back to your mom before she gets into trouble."

Luckily his house hounds had emerged to guard what they considered a delivery on his doorstep. Their deep-throated snarls kept the unsavory away from her limp body.

The boy ran to his mom and threw himself at her, startling Marduke's dogs. He prepared to signal them to not attack, only to stare, dumfounded, as his hounds let the boy by without so much as even a snarl.

Marduke shook his head at them. "What happened to the days when even a fly couldn't get past you?"

One of them farted, but they both managed to look innocent.

"Jerks," he muttered. Kneeling, Marduke scooped Merry into his arms. "Let's get her into a bed so she doesn't wake up sore."

The boy nodded.

And then with a trust that Marduke usually only saw from his hounds, the boy held on to Marduke's coat as they entered the house.

He almost said, *"Welcome home."*

16

MERRY WOKE inside a chamber she didn't recognize and might have panicked if not for the little body pressed against her. Miguel remained with her. It eased her somewhat. No matter what, so long as they were together, she could handle anything.

A wet swipe at her mouth as the dog licked had her gagging and reassessing that thought.

"Ugh. Gross." She would tolerate a lot of things, but puppy slobber between her lips wasn't one of them. When she finished wiping and exclaiming, she glanced at Miguel and would have sworn she caught a ghost of a smile, quickly gone.

She cupped his soft cheek. "Hey, baby. Are you okay?" Because she wasn't sure where she was on that scale at the moment. Discomfited? Definitely. Reevaluating life? Totally.

Upon waking, she remembered everything. She was in Hell. She knew she should have returned that penny she found on the ground as a teenager. See where a life of crime could lead you?

She sat up and stretched. "Whose bed is this?" The room appeared occupied if she went by the clothes draped around the place and the books stacked on the nightstand. She didn't really need to ask to know. "This Marduke's place?"

Miguel nodded.

"Where is he?"

"Right here," the man himself claimed as the door opened, revealing him carrying a tray with two domes and a vase with a single wilted flower. "I thought you might be hungry when you woke."

"Was I out long?"

"About an hour."

"Sorry. It must have been the heat." Look at her lying again. She totally belonged here.

"Meeting the devil for the first time can have that effect."

"Thanks for loaning me your bed."

"Um. Yeah. It's kind of the only nice one around. You can keep using it if you want."

"Oh. Where will you sleep?"

Only as his cheeks turned a ruddy color did she grasp his intent and matched his blush.

Before he could stammer a polite reply that would see him sleeping elsewhere she hastily said, "I don't mind sharing."

Relief eased his face, and his smile was something to melt her heart. Miguel ruined it by climbing over her to get to Marduke, who swung him into his arms. Miguel appeared to have done a bit of an about-face when it came to the big guy.

"I see you two are getting along better."

"We came to an understanding. Little man here was worried when you fainted. You okay?"

"I'm good. I think. If confused. I didn't imagine it. We are in Hell."

"Yes."

"How? I don't remember dying."

"Because you didn't. I brought you through a portal."

She digested that bit. "A portal implies a doorway."

"Yes, only in this case it opens up between dimensions."

"So I went from Earth to Hell without dying and I met the devil." She lay back down. "I think I need another moment." Because her head was spinning.

"Don't you dare. You're stronger than this."

"Am I?" she mused aloud.

"You better be since Lucifer is in the living area determined to finish his welcome."

She bolted upright. "The devil is waiting for me?" She might have squeaked.

His grin widened enough that even with his bristly cheeks, she saw a dimple.

A dimple. Could the man be any hotter? And he wanted to share his bed with her.

"You'll be fine. He just wants to boast a bit. Probably shock you cause that's what he does."

"Why me?"

"You want answers? Go talk to him yourself."

"Can I eat first?" Because in the rush that morning she'd not had anything.

"And make him wait longer?" he asked with an arched brow.

"I'm hungry." And nervous.

"Tardiness is a sin," said the man with the most sinful grin. He revealed the plates under the dome, the pastry unrecognizable, as was the fruit. Or was it a vegetable? She wouldn't know until she ate.

Only she wasn't as hungry as expected. A few

bites and she was chugging the tepid water that tasted lightly of cinnamon. She sighed. "Guess, it's time for my chat with the devil." She slid off the bed, and even before her toes hit the floor, Marduke was there to lend a steadying hand if she needed it.

She tucked her hand against his bicep before it occurred to her. "Hold on. How is it you are acquainted with the devil? And how did you bring us here?"

His lips turned down. "I am in the Dark Lord's employ. I'm his kennel master." Then more softly, "And a demon."

She stared at him as she digested this. Miguel remained tucked against him, trusting. Duke still felt safe to her. What had his words changed?

Nothing.

"Nice to know you're employed. Shall we?"

He had no reply, but he remained close by as they entered the living room and she met the devil for the second time.

"If I say welcome to Hell, will you face plant again?" the devil mocked, not rising from the couch.

"I'm fine now. It's, um, nice to meet you." Another fib and the devil knew it by his smile.

"Where's your baby?" she asked, noting the empty arms and lap.

"Gone down for a nap. If you'd like, I can swap in my son." A flick of his fingers and he had a child playing at his feet with what appeared to be a dinosaur set. A realistic one with motorized parts that moved.

"That's the anti-Christ?" she questioned.

Lucifer rolled his eyes. "Such a dumb name. Why not go with pro-devil? I mean, after all, I made him, and that sop, Jesus Christ, who now likes to be known as Charlie, had fuck all to do with it."

"Um." She really had no clue how to reply to that.

"See, speechless because I'm right. Anyhow, this here is Junior who is close to your runt's age. Now that you're here, we should arrange playdates."

"Um." Speechless still.

"Excellent. Glad you agree. All the experts say socializing is very important at this age."

She woke up enough to finally say, "It's up to Miguel if he wants to play."

Marduke set her child down, and he made a beeline for the pro-devil.

"Have fun!" she called out. How much trouble could they get in with her in the same room?

"Now that the children are taken care of, dear Merry, what a delight to meet you. I have to say, I was tickled red, and not by a latex flog, by your letter to me."

"Letter?" she repeated.

The devil whipped it out, a familiar sheet of paper with a few lines of writing. "'Dear Satan,' that's me, blah blah, I beseech your incredible aid."

"I think I might have spelled something wrong." She bit her lower lip. "I was going for the jolly red fellow."

"Which would have been a waste of your time. Nick is a toymaker, not a life changer. I, on the other hand, can most definitely assist."

Her eyes widened. "Really, you don't have to."

"I insist."

"No, *I* insist. Surely an important person like yourself has better things to do. I don't need your help." She was being rude and ungracious, yet accepting the devil's aid? Surely more wrong.

"Pish. Posh. Crabapple sauce. Your situation is already being handled. Why, because of me, your body isn't cooling in a morgue right now. You just sit back and relax while my man Marduke does all the work."

"Marduke?" She cast him a quick glance. "What's going on?"

"Lucifer, as usual, is being a dumbass. Just ignore him."

"Such disrespect," the devil exclaimed. "Can you see why I hold him in such high esteem?"

She felt herself growing faint again and leaned in to Marduke. He placed an arm around her. "You've had your fun. Go away."

"But I've just arrived!" the devil complained. "And you don't want to see Junior throwing a tantrum because I cut his playdate short."

Only one thing to do. "Why not leave him here for a few hours then? We can handle it."

"We can?" Marduke yelped.

The devil grinned. "Splendid idea, Merry. Maybe I'll take this as a chance to play a round of golf. Or defile my wife. Or both." Lucifer snapped out of sight, and Marduke raised his brows.

"I can't believe you just offered to babysit."

"They're having fun." At least they were until she noticed the dinosaurs were real, with actual hungry mouths and sharp teeth. Miguel held one dangling from his thumb, oblivious to the holes in his skin.

She wrangled the dangerous toys into a box then had the boys playing in the dirt yard under a red ashy sky.

A surprisingly awesome day that got even better in bed that night.

Three times for her.

17

NOW EXPECTING Miguel's early morning wakeup, Marduke rose and dressed before the boy could peek into the room. The previous night, Miguel had followed his puppy to the adjoining chamber for the hounds. The pallets in there were big enough for one little boy and his dog to curl up in. Merry added a blanket, and Marduke gave his house hound companions, Frik and Frak, their orders. "Guard."

They'd die before they let anything hurt the kid.

The boy appeared bright eyed and ready to face the day at Hell's version of predawn, which was like nine a.m. earth time. Marduke put a finger to his lips and then pointed to the bed, where

Miguel's exhausted mother—His fault. *Hehehe*—rested. The boy appeared uncertain, so Marduke held open his arms and Miguel ran to him. Most natural thing in the world and, while new, felt damned right.

He headed for the door, only to feel the boy tense. He noticed his gaze trained on the bed. Speaking might wake her, so he padded over softly so the kid could see she was fine.

Only when Miguel nodded did they leave the room.

In the hall, he could finally speak. "Good boy, letting her sleep. I think she could use it."

The kid agreed.

"Lucky for you, I'm always up early. Gotta tend to the dogs." His older pairfollowed him to the kitchen before flopping in front of the hearth. It might seem odd to have one given Hell was never cold, and yet, how else would they cook? And then there was that one time Hell froze over and he was glad to have it.

The boy, whose puppy stuck close to his side, helped him scoop food into the bowls and only sprayed himself once with the water nozzle before getting it in the right place,

Marduke pointed to a rag. "You can wipe off with that."

Miguel eyed him then the towel. He scrubbed his face dry, leaving the hair by his forehead spiked.

Giving him a nod, Marduke jerked his head. "Gonna help me with the rest?"

A rapid nod and they were off to the kennels, the hounds yipping happily at the sight of him. Only Roisin needed a slap for the way he eyed the kid.

He warned them, "Touch the boy and I will skin you myself."

The kid almost smiled. He'd swear it.

Side by side, they tended the hounds. There weren't as many as they used to have. Back in the day, an average of a hundred filled the place, but that was during a more violent time. Now, they kept fewer than a dozen for the Dark Lord; the rest were adopted out.

The morning chores done, it was time to check on an expecting mother.

"Number one rule, never startle a hound." Marduke crouched by the boy and held out his hand to Morgana, a heavily pregnant bitch who'd taken off the arm of the last fellow who startled her.

Morgana gave him the barest sniff before fixing her beautiful red eyes on the child. She licked her chops.

"Don't you even think of it," Marduke chided. "We don't eat the little ones, remember?"

She definitely rolled her eyes, and the boy by his side gave a little shake. Was he laughing? Nope. A glance showed Miguel serious as ever.

But Marduke understood why now. When Merry had been giving the boy a bath the previous night, he'd made a point of finding out everything he could. Underhanded? Yup. He knew she'd downplay anything bad that had happened to her and the kid. He wanted the truth.

The truth was ugly. Miguel was held at gunpoint during a drug deal that saw his dad shot in front of him. It happened at a holiday parade. The shooter was some gangbanger dressed in a Santa suit. A shitty thing to happen, but at the same time, Miguel's dad, Brian, had asked for it. The Hell records had Brian listed as a petty con artist. Druggie. Thief. A murderer, too, lacing drugs with crap he knew would kill people.

Didn't seem like Merry's type at all.

Then again, she'd had sex with him, and he definitely wasn't her type or even genome. He was one hundred percent demon, but like many of his kind, he preferred to fuck humans. The females tended to be less dangerous. He'd yet to encounter a human female with teeth or traps between her legs. With a demoness? Sometimes you didn't leave with all your body parts intact.

The boy reached out to rub behind Morgana's ear, and soon she was on her side, leg thumping, grunting happily and even drooling. Kid had a knack with hounds. Maybe even a future as his apprentice.

The thought froze him. A future implied he'd be sticking around. Given Miguel's mother's attachment, they came as a package duo. Was he ready for that?

Marduke glanced back to the door leading to the main house. Might not be horrible.

"If you're going to stick around and work for your keep, you'll need a job title."

The boy glanced at him.

"How's assistant to the kennel master?"

The kid's nose scrunched.

"Means you get to help me with these lumps." He grabbed Roisin before his massive head could knock him or the boy over. "Mostly, it involves making sure they're fed and interacted with. Wild hellhounds will kill anyone. Tamed ones? Only those they consider a threat to their friends."

The boy cocked his head in question.

"Well, yeah, they're my friends. And you are, too."

The boy said nothing, but Marduke understood.

"Your mom as well. She's under my protection, which means the hounds will defend her so long as she does no harm to me, them, or the Dark Lord."

The boy's lips pursed.

"Bah, don't let the stories bother you. Don't get me wrong, Lucifer's a dick. He'd sell his own mother if she were still around, and he's got awful taste in clothes, but he ain't all that bad."

A wry expression showed Miguel's doubt.

"You'll see if you stick around." Which might be nice. He enjoyed the kid's company. As for the mother…she wasn't bad. For a lady.

Speaking of whom, she'd snuck up on them. None of his hounds thought to warn him. He frowned at his dogs. The bitch lay there, tongue lolling as the boy continued to pet her. Roisin was no better, not even opening an eye where he lay in Marduke's lap.

"Traitors," he muttered as Merry dropped down beside him on the side not taken up by massive dog.

She appeared more stable now that she'd gotten over her shock at being in Hell. It took some explaining before she'd grasped she wasn't A) dead or B) a cursed soul banished from Heaven. He'd yet to get to the part about no one getting past the pearly gates anymore.

Then last night she'd shone bright as the sun in his arms.

"So this is where you've been hiding. Who is this wondrous creature?" she exclaimed, reaching too quickly, startling Morgana, who snarled.

"Careful," he admonished.

Too late. Merry had her hand out, and Morgana's mouth opened then shut on the treat dropped into it.

"Because of your note, I knew you and Miguel were busy, so I whipped up some doggie biscuits in that marvelous kitchen of yours while having my coffee. It's huge!" she exclaimed.

Back when he had a much larger staff and fuller kennels, it used to be much busier. "You appear recovered." And he didn't just mean from shock. He'd put her through some strenuous attention the night before.

"Meaning I don't look like poop," she said with a giggle and wink at her son. He noticed her pink cheeks.

Miguel pointed to the round belly on Morgana.

"Is she going to have puppies? How exciting." The enthusiasm wasn't faked.

The boy tugged again, and with much pointing and gesturing explained he'd been hired.

Although his excitement paled when Roisin let out a big fart and then proceeded to move not far away to give them a present.

"Better handle it," Marduke said to Miguel, whose eyes widened. He chuckled as he added, "Kennel masters and their assistants don't handle cleanup. That's for the imps. Ring that bell over there." He pointed to a rope, and Miguel couldn't scramble fast enough.

As the boy delegated poop duty, Merry leaned into Marduke. "Thanks."

"For what?"

"For making him happy. I haven't seen him this content in a long time."

"Bah. It was nothing," he blustered.

"To you. To a boy who's had a tough year and his mother, this is paradise. Thank you." She flung her arms around him, and he didn't know what to do but catch her and hug her back.

He welcomed the kiss that pecked his mouth. Then missed her as she bounced away and started chattering a mile a minute to her son, asking to see everything.

The questions didn't stop there. She went after Marduke as well, asked him about the hounds' diets. Then ingredients. Apparently, she thought the dogs would like some home-cooked meals. His hounds needed only one taste to agree.

Spoiled fuckers. Just like their kennel master who got to have her in his arms and bed every night.

The days passed, and there was no talk of her leaving. At all. Suited him just fine. Merry and the boy fit well in his life to the point he didn't want to imagine it without them. She seemed happy, singing in the kitchen as she cooked, animated when reading a story to the kid before bed, bouncing into his lap when the evening arrived and it was time to relax.

Christmas approached, and despite Lucifer's rants and grumbling about the farce being celebrated—the wrong day for the birth of his nephew and the fact his cousin stole it from Lucifer, who was the one to turn it into a marketing, capitalistic wonder—people decorated for the holidays. Lights were strung and attached to imp wheels. For treats, the little bastards would run all night long and keep them lit. While attempts had been made over the years to get true electricity running, the science of Hell made it unstable at best.

Outside the compound, tacky garland hung off of everything. The light displays went from bright to pornographic. Not that Miguel ever saw anything untoward. Marduke always took paths to avoid the worst of it and distracted the boy when there was no choice.

The kid no longer glared at the sight of holiday cheer, which might be why Merry, in a rare moment of shyness, asked, "I don't suppose we could find ourselves a Xmas tree?"

They'd recently learned the boy didn't react aversely to the more generic term. Nor did he seem to mind the Hellish versions of Santa. Biker Santa. Tutu wearing, bold-makeup Santa. Buff and wearing only little red shorts St. Nick. Only roly-poly, jolly Santa Claus caused him to lose his absolute shit. Marduke didn't blame him. He'd met the guy once and hated him. But then again, he hated most people.

"I'm sure we can find something." He would have actually given her anything because of the damned smile she bestowed upon him.

"You are the best!" She threw her arms around Marduke as she exclaimed it.

And it felt good. Fucking good because he absolutely knew, without a doubt, she meant it.

They went to the fifth circle to a store he knew that sold the best artificial trees. In Hell, the plant life endured a precarious existence, and those that survived had to be tough—aka deadly to most other species. So the denizens of the pit tended to avoid anything that might suddenly try and eat them for something they could control. A fake tree could be as wondrous as a real one. Although he would admit some appeared strange.

Merry cocked her head at more than one iteration. She even clung to him at one point as she exclaimed, "That one's made of snakes."

"Very popular with the gorgons and basilisks in Hell." He dropped bits of information all the time, and she soaked it up, not disputing or freaking. She always appeared utterly accepting and had this way of always finding the positive.

"I'll bet it keeps their homes rodent free. How practical."

See? Always half-full. It made him wonder if there was anything that could make her snap.

They wandered the store, Miguel showing more animation than usual. He skipped ahead, the puppy with no name still at his heels. Merry hadn't named it, which was a good thing. Dog belonged to the boy. Boy should name it.

She held his hand, which made his chest swell and his scowl mighty. It kept any of the demons, imps, and even the damned from coming too close. Merry could flit from tree to tree, happily exclaiming over each one.

"Look, Duke"—her nickname for him that used by anyone else would have meant violence—"it's sparkly."

"Nope." A demon had some lines he wouldn't cross even for love.

Love?

He froze, and she had to tug hard before he moved.

When had that happened? It couldn't be. What if she didn't feel the same?

Whack. The wall didn't budge when his head hit it and neither did the thought of love.

"Duke, what are you doing?"

Knocking sense into himself. "Sorry, had something bugging me. Fixed now." Or should he say resigned. He'd fallen for Merry.

"Don't hurt that pretty face." She patted his cheek, and he saw a demon do a double take that made him snarl in his direction. "If you hate glitter that much, then we shall find something more manly. But I draw the line at sharp things, like that dagger tree we saw in the front. I don't want Miguel to get hurt."

"How about we keep looking and see if we find one that seems like it wouldn't suck?"

Her grin was precious as she said, "I think we can manage that."

In the end, Miguel and his dog chose their tree. The duo stood in front of an intricate rendition comprised of building blocks in shades of white and gray hues to a green so dark it almost appeared black. The jagged layer of blocks gave the impression of pine boughs. Cool looking, but he would have preferred the version that didn't have a box saying some assembly required. In Hell, if the instructions claimed it was a one-man job of an hour, you could guarantee that needed to be multiplied by five or more.

Marduke might die before completing it.

So be it.

Merry gestured animatedly. "That is an epic choice. Love it. Can you imagine it by the fireplace? We'll wrap it in glowworms. I saw a store that sells them in all kinds of colors. Maybe we can string some popcorn."

"Easier and cheaper to use hellcorn." Similar in the sense it popped but people didn't usually eat it.

"Good thing you're tall. We'll need your help to crown it. With what?" She tapped her chin.

Miguel rose on his tiptoes and pointed to the glowing pentagram on another tree.

The Dark Lord would be pleased by their choice.

Merry leaned her head against him. It was the best moment ever.

Pity she jinxed it by saying, "It's going to be a great Xmas!"

18

THE TREE DIDN'T EXACTLY PULL TOGETHER quickly. The instructions were terrible, and the small pieces many. Duke's big hands tried, but he lacked the fine dexterity to do it. But he tried along with Miguel, after they shooed Merry away, saying it was man's work.

It melted something inside her to see the two of them, heads bent together. While they bonded, Merry baked. A roast of something that smelled good for dinner and some cookies. Gingerbread men that giggled and wiggled inside the cookie tin. The imps outside the kennel compound, waiting for odd jobs, were glad to help in exchange for her baking. By the time they woke Christmas Eve, the building block tree was done and ready to decorate.

The glowworms went on nicely, and puppy only got two in its fur. Duke had no problem placing the star at the top. The hellcorn she strung draped perfectly.

They left, and she tapped her lower lip as she eyed the tree. Almost perfect. It needed just one more thing.

Tinsel. Something gaudy to shock Duke. Once she got the idea, she had to follow through, giggling already at his expected expression. She went by her room and grabbed the brooch he'd given her the previous day, which he said people would treat as money when it came to shopping.

"Jewelry? Does this mean we're going steady?" she'd teased.

The gruff demon blushed. "It'll keep you safe. Anyone tries and bother you, make sure they see it."

Because he would protect her. He'd then proceeded to take her to the nearest store so she'd know its location. She had a feeling it was to also scowl at people and let them know in advance, mess with her, mess with him. It was ridiculously masculine and cute.

She exited the compound and headed for the

equivalent of the corner store at the border of the first and second ring. It was one of her favorite places to wander since Marduke first took her.

The store sold the groceries and junk food you expected, if by different brands and names, but it also had weirder stuff, too, like eyeballs floating in liquid that could be used as a security system. If you were willing to pop them in and out of your own head.

No thanks.

The brooch didn't just serve as a credit card; it also served as warning, ensuring no one bothered her. This wasn't the first time she'd popped out to the store. But it was the first time someone accosted her by name.

"Merry, is that you?"

In that moment, she did a very un-Merry-like thing. She turned around and ran away.

What am I doing?

Running away from Brian, Miguel's dead daddy. Still dead but living in Hell. A place that must be rubbing off because her uncharitable ass wanted nothing to do with him.

As far as she was concerned, she'd be just fine never seeing him again. Let him rot for everything he'd done.

Followed by immediate guilt; after all, Brian was Miguel's dad. Her child remained traumatized to this day by his father's death. Would meeting his damned soul make things better or worse?

I'm a terrible person. It shouldn't even be a question. Some would say Brian had a right to see his son. She shouldn't be so selfish. Especially given how happy she was. She might currently live in Hell, but with Marduke, it became paradise. He was attentive to her needs, treated her so kindly, and his passion for her and her pleasure...

Then there was how he bonded with her son. She might have worried about his abrupt manner, and the way he set boundaries, but it seemed to be working. Miguel had been a thousand times less temperamental of late.

Did she want to tilt that precarious achievement?

It was the devil, of all people, that showed her the answer. He appeared, as usual, without warning, a hint of brimstone the only clue he'd arrived.

She no longer startled, nor was she surprised to have a child thrust at her. The girl. With the sweetest fire-imbued eyes and a charming chortle.

Jujube snuggled against her, and for a second,

Merry thought it would be nice to have another kid.

With Marduke.

He'd make an amazing father. The question being, did he want a family? He never really spoke of the future or what he wanted from Merry.

"My lovely Merry, quite contrary, how does your garden grow?" A valid question since Marduke had brought her soil from Earth and seeds so she could try her hand at growing fresh vegetables, a scarce commodity in Hell. Given how long that might take, it implied her being around for a while.

"It's coming along. We've had to adjust the light source a few times. And one of the seedlings went rogue." It literally grew legs and ran away. But that was Hell for you.

"And how is that fine son of yours?"

"Good."

"So you're happy?"

"Yes." Spoken very slowly.

"You're welcome." Lucifer extended his arms, showing off his strange gray shirt that appeared webbed from arm to the torso, the fabric patterned to appear as feathers. The neckline gaped, showing off a thick chain, the pendant set with a giant unblinking eye.

Unnerving. She turned away. "Excuse me, but what am I welcome for?"

"That I answered your letter, of course."

"The one meant for Santa."

"You say that now, and yet subconsciously you knew that twat couldn't help and so, instead, you sent it to me." Lucifer jabbed his chest. "A smart move since I gave you what you asked for."

"How do you figure that?"

"Are you going to tell me the boy isn't better off?"

"Better, yes, but he's still not smiling or talking." She'd take even a smirk.

"Semantics. The boy is good. You're good. Cough it up."

"I don't know what you think I owe you. I never agreed to anything." She knew enough of Hell's rules to know both parties had to agree to a tit-for-tat bargain.

"Welshing on our deal?" The devil grabbed his chest and almost poked the eye on the amulet, which somehow managed to glare. "I'm shocked, Merry. But rather pleased. I knew being here would be a bad influence on you. I'm good at spotting the evil in people."

Evil? It horrified Merry to realize that, despite her religious upbringing, she was happily living in sin. Conducting sin. Embracing it.

And loving it.

What did that say about her?

"So what is it exactly that you want?"

"Your soul. Duh." The devil didn't just roll his eyes; his whole head rolled too.

"Don't I have to die to give you my soul?"

"This might come as a surprise, Merry, but everyone dies."

"What if I don't want to?"

"Then don't die. I can wait."

Wait because he knew her soul would end up being sent to him. Was that such a bad thing? She was happy here. Why would she want anything else?

As they walked, they ended up outside the compound holding the kennels. High walls protected the citizens of Hell. According to Marduke, the hounds only rarely escaped since they made the walls more than thirty feet high.

"If I'm going to be yours, no matter what, then why do you want me to say you can have my soul?"

"Something official for the record. Dots and slashes and all that." He grinned, that of a shark in a suit, a handsome one who oozed trust.

"Can I think about it?" She wanted to run it by Marduke.

"Don't wait too long." The devil held out his arms for the baby, who floated back to him. She sneezed in his face. Flames licked his skin. He chuckled. "Daddy's girl." And popped out of sight.

Merry wasn't sure she'd ever get used to the fact the devil had not only chatted with her in person but trusted her with his child. Did that make her his handmaiden? Please don't let his wife get ideas. The tell-all book, *Mother Earth and the Bodies Buried Within the Garden*, hinted at those who disappeared after showing too much interest in her husband.

When she'd asked Marduke about the veracity of the claims, all he'd said was, "You should see her roses."

"Merry?"

Uh-oh. The devil appearing had made her forget her real problem.

Brian stood in front of her, looking expectant. How had she not seen past his shallow good looks to the rot inside?

Which led to her remembering how the devil said she was bad enough to merit the pit. It seemed impossible. Her mom raised her to be a good religious girl. Now she was a woman who'd had a child out of wedlock and lived in sin with a demon.

Who was the real Merry? And what did she want?

Time to find out.

19

"You might want to hustle. Your woman is chatting it up with another dude." The devil suddenly appeared in the kennel and almost got punched.

"What did I tell you about apparating in here?"

"I'm the Dark Lord. I go wherever, whenever. One of the job perks."

"Then use it to poof elsewhere." He finished brushing Terror's fur and closed the door to his suite. Each hound had more than a single room. They were treated quite well. Better than most of Hell's denizens, actually.

"I will leave once you do something about Merry."

"She's allowed to talk to men." Even if he didn't like it.

"Even this man?" The devil glanced around furtively before whispering, "Her ex."

The brush in his hand cracked as his fingers tightened. "Nothing wrong with them catching up." What he didn't know was how she felt about Brian. His understanding was they weren't together when the guy died, but was that by choice? Did she still love him? Would she want to go back to her ex? Who'd want a grumpy bastard like him?

"Ah, I see you finally grasp what I'm saying. I'm going to leave now."

Of course, the devil would now that he'd sown his seed of chaos. Maybe he lied, though.

"Frik and Frak, watch the boy."

Miguel was grooming Morgana. Marduke bolted from the kennel, running for the front door. He swung it open in time to see Merry walking away from someone.

Smiling.

Happy about something. Probably the reunion. Knowing he was about to get dumped might have made him a tad surly as she neared and chirped,

"You'll be glad to know I changed my mind and didn't buy the sparkly garland."

"You don't have to lie." They might be in Hell, but not everything had to be about kissing the Dark Lord's ass.

A frown wrinkled her usually perfect brow. "What is wrong with you?"

"I know you found Brian." The name left a sour taste in his mouth.

"More like he found me."

"I guess you'll be taking Miguel and leaving." He said it low and pathetic. He couldn't help it. His heart? It shattered into dust.

"Leave? Never. I want to be with you," she stated. Quite firmly as a matter of fact.

His heart paused its destruction. "What of Brian?"

"He and I were done a long time ago. The only reason we saw each other was Miguel. That's why he came looking for me. Brian wants to see him."

"And what did you say?" Because she'd seemed happy walking back, which made no sense.

She bit her lip before angling her chin and saying, "I said no. He's never been a good influence on Miguel. Actually, I'm going to say it; Brian was a terrible father."

"Brian hurt him?" He growled, ready to mete out some violence.

She shook her head. "I never saw a mark on him, and I asked. Miguel said no. Nothing else. But there's other ways of harming. The name-calling. The neglect. I tried to be nice, after all this was Miguel's dad, and the courts said he could have Miguel on weekends. But I hated it. And now he thinks just because we're both in Hell he can demand access." She tossed her head. "I said no."

"How'd he take it?"

"Not well. Started threatening me and stuff."

"What?" he bellowed.

"Right? That was my reaction, too. I told Brian if he had a problem to take it up with you. That my big boyfriend was meaner than him and he'd make his time in Hell thus far seem like a cakewalk."

Boyfriend. His chest swelled. "You told him that?" He melted. Like his heart seriously became a giant puddle.

"You might not be a man of many words, Duke, but your actions say it all. You love me."

Something inside him burst as the pressure of holding it in eased. "Fuck me, but I do. I'd do anything for you."

"Anything?" she purred, running her finger down his chest.

Which was when they were interrupted by the baying of hounds.

20

THE URGENCY in the howling had them racing for the kennel.

"Why are they freaking?" she asked. Then in the same breath, "Where's Miguel?"

"Boy is with them, and they'd only be howling if one of them was in danger." Not reassuring. Especially matched with Marduke's grim expression.

"How can they be in danger? The compound is secure."

"But not impenetrable."

Her heart sank as it occurred to her there were only a few hounds that wandered loose. Frik, Frak, and Miguel's pup.

"Miguel!" she yelled the moment they entered the kennel.

The dogs were going nuts, slamming into their doors.

Marduke didn't stop but kept running for the far end. "I can smell the road outside. Someone opened the gate."

Panic set in, fast and furious. Especially since she knew who was just outside. Had Miguel seen him? Or worse, had Brian, that slimy jerk, kidnapped her kid?

At the far end of the kennels, the service door was ajar, a hound lying in its opening, its muzzle covered in a yellow dust.

"Sleeping powder. Someone knocked out my dogs." Marduke's voice was tight as he paused only a second to put a hand on them and check their breathing. Frak lay in the door, Frik just outside.

And as if finding them were a signal, the baying hounds ceased.

Merry glanced up and down the street and saw no one at first. It was Marduke who pointed. "Follow the powder."

A dusting of yellow led them down the street, past nice houses—this was after all the first ring, home of the most honored in Lucifer's circle. But even the rich had their problems. Alleys and basements that catered to the less savory.

It was down some slimy steps they found him.

Brian, clutching a bleeding leg. The culprit at his feet.

Miguel's puppy was covered in that drugging dust.

"You!" she huffed. "What have you done with my son?"

"He's mine, too."

She didn't have to say or do a thing. Marduke had Brian by the neck and slammed him against the wall.

She stood in front of him, arms crossed. "I said, where is my son?"

"Doing something for his daddy," Brian choked out. "No big deal. He was happy to help."

"You lured him outside. Drugged the dogs protecting him. Where is he now?"

"With Santa."

A smarmy reply that saw him slammed into the wall a few more times until he blubbered. "This isn't my fault. The kid brought it on himself. If Miguel hadn't spooked him in the first place, I wouldn't have died, and everything would have gone off without a hitch."

"Meaning what?" She'd never spoken so dully, so coldly. Marduke cast her a glance.

But she focused on Brian. A man she should have never gotten involved with. A loser she'd given one too many chances.

"I owed money, and they wouldn't give me any more pills without payment. So I found something they wanted."

Her eyes widened as it occurred to her what he admitted. "You sold our son for drugs?"

"They were just going to borrow him for the weekend."

She punched him.

Right in the nose. It broke. It bled. Brian cried, and she didn't care.

She'd hauled off to hit him again when Marduke growled, "What's your death have to do with the boy now?"

"Apparently, Gitmo"—the name of the fake Santa drug dealer who'd died that night— "claims the debt is still owed with interest, given how it turned out."

Wham. Marduke hit him this time, and Brian didn't get back up.

A chill filled her that no heat of Hell could fix.

"Oh no. No. No." She paced. "How could he do this?"

"They can't have gone far. Come. We'll find him." Marduke scooped up the puppy and shoved it into his pocket then held out his hand, and she clasped it.

As they exited the stairwell, Marduke whistled and called the hounds by name. "Terror and Poe, Merlyn and Goshen. Stupid and Dumbass, and I guess you, too, you smelly fucker Roisin."

The Kennel Master must have some kind of magic because, despite having left them locked in their rooms, the hounds answered his call. They flowed down the street, slavering and slobbering, their red eyes wild. Frik and Frak, a little slower and groggier, brought up the rear of the pack.

Marduke whistled at the old pair and pointed to where they'd left Brian. "Take him to the prison, and you don't have to be gentle about it."

She'd have sworn the dogs smiled as they went about their task. She shut her ears to the screams that erupted. Couldn't happen to a more deserving guy.

Wild-eyed, Marduke bared his teeth, and for the first time, she saw the demon as he said, "Now we hunt."

21

Marduke held her by the hand as they chased after the hounds. He didn't worry about losing them, being connected on a level most people couldn't achieve. Between Marduke and his hounds, they'd find the boy.

The scent of the kid led the way because someone forgot to mask it. Obviously, the person who came after the boy was new. Because only an idiot would A) ever attack the kennel, B) kidnap a child, and C) piss Marduke off.

But now add D) to the mix. They took away Merry's smile.

How dare they?!

The trail left the first ring for the second and headed for the loud cacophony that turned out to be a parade. A Christmas one with the most garish of floats.

His dogs weren't distracted, and as people realized the hounds were loose, the joyful cries of celebrations turned to screams, then a stampede out of the dogs' path. Which made it easier to see the guy in the Santa suit, yanking Miguel by the arm. The boy kept digging in his heels and looking behind.

Which meant, as the crowd thinned, he noticed Marduke. Hope shone in the boy's eyes.

Fake Santa saw him coming, too, and cuffed the kid.

"I am going to tear out your spine and beat you with it, fucker." Marduke ran, and people dove out of his way.

Fake Santa didn't give up. He dragged the kid into an alley.

Bad idea.

The hounds followed, and then there was much screaming. By the time they entered the alley, the dogs were carrying off bits of the damned soul.

It wouldn't kill the guy. Not in Hell. He'd eventually be put back together so the devil could punish him again and again, the sentence now longer with the added infractions.

The boy sat huddled on the ground, knees tucked, hugging them.

Merry ran past Marduke and dropped to her knees. "Baby. Are you all right?" She palpated the kid before dragging him into her arms.

"Stop smothering him," Marduke drawled as the boy sent him a glance that screamed, *Help.*

"I was so worried," she wailed. "It's my fault. I'm never letting him out of my sight again."

"Calm your tits, Merry, and let the boy go before you Norman Bates him for life."

She turned a glare on him. "Don't you tell me how to parent."

"I will if you're being crazy. The boy is fine."

"He was just kidnapped! He is not fine."

"You're right. He's worried about this."

Marduke pulled out the puppy, who yawned and worked its chops, still under the influence of the drug. But Miguel beamed and shoved away from his mother, reaching for his companion.

She pursed her lips and might have complained more if the boy hadn't looked at her, his arms full of dog, and smiled.

Merry burst into tears.

22

MERRY MANAGED to stop crying by the time they got back home.

Home being the kennel compound in Hell with Marduke.

What could have been an epic nightmare turned out to be the best thing ever. Miguel was safe. His dad and that bad Santa were no longer a threat. And even better, Marduke had said he loved her.

This was turning out to be the best Christmas ever.

A tired Miguel went to bed early, leaving her alone with Marduke in the living area. He sat on the couch and tugged her into his lap.

"Busy day."

"Terrifying," she admitted, leaning against him.

"If it helps, I've had new security placed on the gates and the Alchemists Guild is working on a charm to prevent the dogs from being drugged again."

"You've thought of everything."

Even a present for Miguel. The bike with its massive bow waited under the tree for her child. She'd also spotted a small box in the branches of the tree. The kind that screamed jewelry.

She kissed him. "Thank you."

"Don't thank me. I would do anything for you."

"Anything?" she teased.

She rose from his lap, only to sink to the floor between his knees.

"What are you doing?" he asked, leaning back on the couch, regarding her through half-mast eyes.

"Giving you an early Xmas gift." She winked as she tugged his pants down.

The smart man didn't argue but helped them both strip so that he could continue to watch as she grabbed hold of him. His thick cock pulsed in her grip.

A lick of the top showed him salty and sweet. Just the way she loved him.

She kissed his shaft. Licked it, her tongue running from the head all the way down and back up.

Duke made a noise, and his head went back. His hands gripped the sofa cushion as she sucked, taking him deep, suctioning hard. The flat edges of her teeth grazed his velvety skin.

"Merry." He groaned her name.

She kept sucking.

"Merry. Stop. I'm going to come."

She was well aware he would, and she caught it—every last drop—and swallowed. Because everyone knew the difference between love and like.

And she kept playing until his hips jerked and he gasped, "You're going to kill me."

"Would you prefer I do this instead?" She crawled onto the couch on hands and knees, wiggling her ass at him.

"Fuck yeah." He covered her, his body draping over hers as he kissed his way down her back, nipped her buttocks, and then licked her until she came.

And then while she was still coasting from her oral orgasm, he thrust into her. His thick shaft was oh so welcome. Filling. She cried out and rocked her hips, pushing against him, wanting him deep.

Deeper.

He growled and rumbled as he thrust, his pace steady and perfect, hitting her in that sweet spot over and over until she shattered.

But she remembered to exclaim, before they collapsed in a heap, "I love you."

Those three words saw her getting two more presents that night. The last one ended in the shower, where the tile wall held her upright because her legs weren't sure they wanted to work.

She smiled at him as they put on some clothes. A clock struck twelve, and tugging her pants up, she grinned and said, "Merry Christmas."

His eyes crinkled at the corners and his cheek dimpled as he said, "You are the best present ever."

She might have giggled and preened at his praises if not for the sudden shriek!

"Miguel!"

They emerged from the bathing chamber to find a fat man in a red suit, his beard tangled, his nose bulbous, and his cheeks florid, standing by the bed. Miguel sat in it, looking terrified, arms around the dog that still didn't have a name. Puppy's hackles were up, and it growled in a low tone. It wasn't alone. Frik and Frak flanked the fat man.

"Who are you?" she exclaimed. "Get away from my son."

"Call off the dogs!" the guy demanded.

"They're just doing their job," Marduke drawled.

"And so am I. Or don't you recognize me? I'm Santa."

"You?" She eyed him dubiously. He was more unkempt than she'd expected, more drunken-vagrant looking than jolly.

"In the flesh, Merry. So glad I finally found you. I am here to fix the snafu with your letter."

The letter? She shook her head. "No thanks. I'm good."

Santa looked around. "I think your definition of good needs help. Or have you missed the fact you're in Hell?"

"Well aware." She tucked closer to Marduke. "And totally fine with it. Really. You can go."

Santa didn't like that, and his lips flattened.

"Suit yourself." He turned to Miguel. "What about you, son? You going to turn down something from Santa? Mind you, it's not that bike you asked for. You weren't exactly good this year." The fat man pulled something from his sack and dropped it onto the bed.

"Excuse me?" Merry huffed. "He's been great considering everything he's been through."

"Breaking things. Temper tantrums. Being disrespectful." Santa ticked off the supposed infractions. "Rules is rules. Bad kids get coal."

Sure enough, a lump sat on the bed. Merry stared at it and then Santa, who had the nerve to deliver the insult to her kid in person.

Disparaging *my* baby. Her gaze narrowed.

Marduke snorted. "Oh, Nick. You did not just do that."

Before Merry could go mama bear on Santa's ass, Miguel shifted, leaning forward to grab the coal. He studied it then the man in the red suit.

Miguel tossed it to the side and then smiled—a big, beautiful thing—before saying clearly, "Bad Santa. Go."

The command wasn't for the fat man but a dog, who obeyed. The hound came off that bed without a sound and its mouth open wide.

"Don't you dare. Call it off. That's it, you're on the naughty list forever!" Santa went hustling for the air duct he must have popped out of. Lost the ass of his pants during his escape.

But who cared about the fact they'd never leave cookies for the fat bastard again.

Shock had her jaw hanging open as Miguel spoke again. "Good girl."

Girl?

Duke leaned close and whispered, "Did I mention the fact the dogs will adopt the gender of whatever their master will respond to best."

"No, you forgot that part," she muttered as she approached her son, trying to not be too giddy at the fact he'd spoken.

Miguel hugged his dog and rubbed his face in her fur before saying, "Spot." The most perfect name ever for the solid-colored Hellhound.

"Merry Xmas, Miguel." Because it might be early, but the big day had come.

As expected, he loved the bike and the set of mini dinosaurs the devil sent over. Merry got a pendant and a gruff, "It says you're the Kennel Mistress."

Which was kind of like a proposal and almost the best gift she got that day.

The very best thing happened when Miguel flung his arms around her and said, "Love you, Mama."

Duke hugged Merry close as she sobbed happily. "Thank you, Satan, for this Xmas miracle."

EPILOGUE

CHRISTMAS MORNING PASSED in a blur as Lucifer sat on the couch beside his wench. The children were playing with the boxes discarded throughout his kingdom, because they already had every toy in existence.

Lucifer had an inter-world videoconference coming up shortly with his children. Muriel mostly, since Bambi had been distant of late. He'd even invited his short-lived son, Chris. After all, the boy was still a relation.

It was a good day. He basked in the greed. The turkey dinner family fights. The way he'd foiled his cousin.

And he mulled his plan to ensure Nick never forgot it.

His notebook sat in his lap. He'd had it for a long time, and it contained random musings from the times he felt contemplative. Artistic.

Gaia patted his leg. "I haven't given you your gift yet."

"Will I blow harder than that volcano in the Atlantic?"

"Later, yes. But right now, I am going to give you the ultimate gift." She leaned close and whispered, "You were right. You knew exactly what Merry needed."

Hell yeah, he did, because the Dark Lord was the most awesome. The smartest. And best dressed.

He kicked off his slippers and shoved his feet into his wife's lap. He should mention they were huge, just like other parts of him.

"You want me to rub them now?" she complained.

"I won the bet."

"By a fluke. I can't believe Marduke fell so quick and that Merry actually gave you her soul."

"I've got a knack for knowing what people want, you know."

"What else are you good at?" Gaia purred.

"I am an epic rhymer. Check out the piece I intend to read at next year's Hellmas special."

> *'Twas that horrible time called Christmas, and all throughout Hell,*
> *Perversion was happening, crime was up as well.*
> *The damned were hanging by their fingers and toes,*
> *Waiting for Satan to cause them some woe.*
>
> *The spawn were alive, and not killed in their crib,*
> *While visions of rampaging filled their little heads.*
> *Gaia in a gown of snowflakes, Lucifer in a dashing ducky suit*
> *Had just settled in for a night of orgasmic sploosh.*
>
> *When inside the chimney, there arose a mighty curse,*
> *As Santa got caught in a fiery burst.*
> *Away to the fireplace, Satan flew like a devil,*

Lit off a rocket, because he's just that evil.

The moon of Santa's ass shone like icky fresh snow,
And gave a red-eyed wink to Lucifer below.
Then, what to his wondering eyes should appear
But an army of elves, brandishing spears.

With a mighty fart and a shimmer of his hips,
Down the chimney came the devil's cousin. Fucking St. Nick.
Lucifer had a plan, and he put it in play.
He yodeled, he commanded, he called them to slay.

"Now, Terror and Poe, Merlyn and Goshen.
On Stupid and Dumbass, and don't forget that smelly cunt, Roisin.
To me, to the chimney, to the roof, and do hurry.

*Don't let him escape, or I'll make you
 adorably furry.*

*As the minions before a raging Lucifer
 do fly
When they meet with his displeasure rise
 to the sky,
To the top of the castle, the hounds they
 trotted,
To threaten a Cousin Nick, soon to be
 departed.*

*In a huff of brimstone, the devil was on
 the roof,
Grinning at the pawing of hounds as
 they harassed those with hooves.
As he waved his hand and prepared to
 astound,
That idiot Nick attacked with a bound.*

*He'd dressed all in pleather, from his
 head to his foot,
But Lucifer looked better in his Darth
 Vader suit.
He did envy the whip Nick kept strapped
 to his waist.*

It reminded him of a battle in another place.

Nick's eyes how they wrinkled as his grimace deepened.
His lips pulled taut, and the effect was cheapened.
He had a boring face and a keg of a belly
That shook when he harangued, proving he was jelly.

A wave of the devil's hand sent Nick to his knees.
All the whining did nothing. He ignored the pitiful pleas.
"You're an ass and a chump," Lucifer declared,
While slicking back his thick and lustrous hair.

The devil spoke many words as he went straight to his work,
Concocting a binding contract that Nick signed with a jerk.
A few drops of blood, because that made it official,

*And Lucifer gave Nick a nod and had it
 sent to judicial.*

*With one final sob, Nick sprang to his
 sleigh,
A coward who'd lost once more to team
 Baphomet.
The nine circles heard the devil exclaim
 as he portaled out of sight,
"Gaia, I fucked over Christmas, expect
 epic screwing tonight!"*

Yeah. Welcome to my twisted version of holiday Hell fun. I hope you had as much fun reading as I did writing it. Merry Xmas.

Find more Hell and other books at EveLanglais.com

www.ingramcontent.com/pod-product-compliance
Ingram Content Group UK Ltd.
Pitfield, Milton Keynes, MK11 3LW, UK
UKHW042001230426
12048UKWH00009B/474